Can a ghost get sick?

"Something's wrong," Callie whispered. "What is it?" The horse's coat was dull, and her eyes were running. More than anything, Star looked tired—and she'd never looked tired, not in all the nights that Callie had ridden her.

Callie took Star's head in her hands, half hoping that if she stared at the horse long enough, she'd figure out what to do. As she stared, Star's ears began to shimmer, so brightly that Callie could see right through them. The shimmering spread through the horse's head, out toward her mane. Callie caught her breath. She'd never seen Star disappear, not while she was still with her. Star's jaw dissolved beneath Callie's hands, leaving her holding only shimmering air. Star's thoughts weakened, too, slowly fading out of Callie's mind.

"No!" Callie screamed. She had the sudden awful feeling that if Star disappeared now, she'd never see her again.

**Look for these other *Phantom Rider* books
from Scholastic!**

Ghost Horse

The Haunted Trail

Ghost Vision

by
Janni Lee Simner

A GLC Book

AN
APPLE
PAPERBACK

SCHOLASTIC INC.
New York Toronto London Auckland Sydney

No part of this publication may be reproduced in whole or in part, or stored in a retrieval system, or transmitted in any form or by any means, electronic, mechanical, photocopying, recording, or otherwise, without written permission of the publisher. For information regarding permission, write to Scholastic Inc., 555 Broadway, New York, NY 10012.

ISBN 0-590-67315-7

Copyright © 1996 by General Licensing Company, Inc. All rights reserved. Published by Scholastic Inc. APPLE PAPERBACKS and the APPLE PAPERBACKS logo are registered trademarks of Scholastic Inc. Cover art copyright © 1996 by General Licensing Company, Inc.

This book is a work of fiction. Names, characters, places, and incidents are products of the author's imagination or are used fictitiously. Any resemblance to actual events, locales, or persons, living or dead, is entirely coincidental.

12 11 10 9 8 7 6 5 4 3 2 1   6 7 8 9/9 0 1/0

Printed in the U.S.A.   40

First Scholastic printing, November 1996

To Mom and Dad,
for raising me in a house full of books

Chapter One

They were going to dig up Star's corral.

Callie lay sprawled across her bed, staring out the window. Workers moved through her yard and across a circle of trampled dirt, talking loudly, while a light wind blew up clouds of dust around them. Sweat plastered their damp shirts to their skin. One of the workers pulled a tape measure from her belt every so often; another held a pad on which he made notes. They were examining the land, so they could give Callie's dad an estimate on building the pool and deck he'd designed. Two other companies had already done the same thing.

Around the workers, small cacti and bushes lay in piles, waiting to be thrown out. Callie had pulled up most of the plants herself, in return for being allowed to take horseback riding lessons. Some taller trees—a green-barked palo verde, several dry yellow-green cottonwoods, a couple of tiny-leaved mesquites—had been left alone. A few rusted fences also remained in the yard; Mom and Dad had decided to let whichever company built the pool handle those.

Farther away, beyond the yard and over the Catalina Mountains, clouds were piling up. The air felt warm and sticky, even with the air conditioner running full blast. Callie's short hair stuck to her scalp, and sweat trickled down her bare neck. Tucson, like the rest of the Sonoran Desert, was only humid when there was rain around.

It wasn't like having a pool wouldn't be great on a day like today. Callie just wished they would dig it somewhere else.

She sighed. To be fair, the workers didn't know they were digging up a corral. Neither did Callie's parents. They knew that the house had once been a ranch, back around the end of World War II; but unlike Callie, they'd never actually seen that ranch. They hadn't dreamed about it, night after night, hadn't seen the ranch's horses running where the workers walked now.

They hadn't met Star.

The workers left the corral and crossed the yard to examine the wash—or dry riverbed—at the edge of the property. Callie rolled onto her back and stared up at the ceiling.

Star was a ghost, the ghost of a horse who had died half a century ago. When Callie had first moved from Long Island to Tucson, she'd hated the desert, but discovering Star had changed that. Now she loved the huge blue sky and stark mountains. And she and Star had become incredibly close. Callie couldn't imagine not having met the horse now.

Someone knocked on Callie's door. "Come in!" she called, sitting up.

Amy Ryan opened the door, wearing a wide-brimmed straw hat and balancing a plate of cookies on one hand. She stepped inside and pulled the door closed behind her. Amy lived across the street from Callie; they'd become good friends that summer.

"Your mom said to bring these in with me." Amy set the plate beside Callie on the bed; the cookies smelled of chocolate, only more bitter. She took off her hat, shook her black hair out of her face, and collapsed into the chair across from Callie, stretching her lanky legs out in front of her. Sweat trickled down the side of her neck. "It sure is sticky out there. I don't know how you stood it out East, where it's so damp all the time."

Callie smiled. When she'd arrived in Tucson, she'd wondered how anyone stood it out West, where the summer—and autumn and spring, too, from what she'd been told—were always so hot and dry.

She reached down and took a cookie off the plate. "So how was school shopping?"

"Fine." Amy picked up a cookie herself. "Josh is so funny when he takes me shopping, though. He always seems kind of embarrassed, especially when we get to looking for clothes. He just stays near the front of the store and tells me to let him know when I'm done." Josh was Amy's brother; he'd raised her ever since their parents had died in a car crash two years before. Josh was also Callie's riding instructor at Sonoran Stables.

Callie bit into her cookie. It tasted weird, sort of like coffee. She scrunched up her face.

"Mocha chip," Amy told her. "Your mom said she was feeling experimental."

Callie put her cookie back down, just as Amy reached for another.

"So how's Rusty doing?" Callie asked. Rusty was Josh's horse, whom he boarded at the stables.

Amy frowned at that. "Rusty's leg is still pretty sore," she said, "but Josh thinks the swelling's finally going down. Not as fast as he'd like, of course."

Callie sighed, knowing Rusty's injury was, in a way, Star's fault. Three weeks before, Josh had taken Callie, Amy, and Callie's older sister, Melissa, riding in the mountains. Star had been fiercely jealous when she'd seen Callie riding one of Sonoran Stables' horses, and so she'd spooked the trail horses, badly enough that they all threw their riders and ran off. Star knew better than that now; Callie didn't think she'd do anything like that again.

When the trail horses had eventually been found, they'd seemed all right. But the next day, Rusty began limping, and Josh found some cactus spines embedded deep in the horse's leg. They came out easily enough, but then Rusty's leg began to swell. Since some spines were poisonous to horses—something Callie hadn't known until Josh had told her—he was pretty worried. And all he could do was put cold packs on the leg, give Rusty some medicine prescribed by the vet, and hope the swelling would go down.

"The thing is," Amy said, munching on a cookie, "Josh would be worried about any injured horse, but because it's *his* horse, he's more worried than usual. And he can't stop wondering how the horses got spooked in the first place." Josh had told his boss a rattlesnake spooked them—reasonable enough, since he'd seen a couple of rattlers near the trail—but he'd never really believed that excuse himself. Since he didn't know about Star, though, he hadn't been able to think of any better explanation.

Amy set the cookie in her hand aside. "Josh has been asking me lots of questions about that ride, trying to figure out what really happened. He thinks it's somehow his fault that the horses all bolted." She bit her lip. "He feels so bad about it that sometimes I wonder if we shouldn't just tell him."

"Amy!" They couldn't tell Josh—or anyone else—about Star. Callie had trusted Amy with Star's secret almost from the start and had reluctantly told her sister later on, but she didn't want anyone else to know. "We can't tell him," Callie said. If too many people knew about Star, word would begin to get out, and who knew what would happen then?

"You're right, of course," Amy said. Her face turned thoughtful. "It's just that I hate seeing Josh all stressed out, you know?"

Callie wasn't sure she did know, but she didn't say so aloud. How could Amy think about talking to Josh about Star, even if she did get along with her brother so much better than most kids got along with their families? Callie had only considered telling her own parents once, not long after discovering Star, and she'd quickly changed her mind. It wasn't as though knowing a ghost was hanging around was likely to make Josh worry less, anyway. Callie knew her parents would only worry more if they knew something like that.

She looked away from Amy and out the window again. The workers were heading back toward the house now. As Callie watched, Melissa walked into the yard with a plate of cookies and a pitcher of water. Melissa's red curls were perfectly in place, her makeup neat and unaffected by the heat. As she offered iced tea and cookies to the workers, she smiled in the syrupy way that always seemed so fake to Callie. Melissa was fifteen; the youngest of the workers was probably only a few years older than that.

Amy followed Callie's gaze outside. "I bet Melissa will be glad when school begins," she said, dropping the subject of Star completely. "Meet some guys her own age for once." One of the guys Melissa had been interested in that summer was Josh, even though he was almost ten years older than she was.

Callie sighed. "I'm not so sure I'm ready for school. Not tomorrow, anyway." Besides, once school started, there wouldn't be as much time to ride Star. Once the pool was in, there wouldn't be as much space, either.

"I know I'm ready for school," Amy said. "It's been ages since I've seen everyone, you know?"

Callie turned to face her friend. They'd spent so much time together that summer that Callie had almost forgotten Amy must have plenty of other friends back at school. Maybe Amy wouldn't want anything to do with Callie once they got there. "I guess you'll be pretty busy

with your regular friends, won't you?" Callie
said.

"What do you mean?" Amy squinted at Callie, looking confused. Then, without warning,
she started laughing. "You're not worried I'm
going to ignore you, are you? You're one of my
regular friends, too, you know. One of my
best friends."

Callie glanced down, embarrassed. By now
she ought to know Amy wouldn't just abandon
her, not for school or for anything else, any
more than Amy would talk about Star if asked
not to. "It's just that I won't know anyone,"
Callie said. She was starting a new school,
after all, and since she was going into seventh
grade, it was her first year of middle school,
as well.

"So?" Amy shrugged. "I'll introduce you to
people. You'll meet people on your own, too."

"I guess." Callie was still worried, though.

Outside, Melissa and the workers had both
left. The sun was out of sight on the other side
of the house, and the few trees cast long shadows across the yard. Callie and Amy sat in silence for a while. Callie had never been able
to just sit like that, not needing to talk, with
any of her friends in New York.

"Are you going to see Star tonight?" Amy
asked after a few minutes.

Callie smiled. "I hope so."

"She really is a beautiful horse," Amy said. "I hope I can see her again, someday."

"Me too," Callie said, though she didn't know when. The reason most people didn't know about Star was that normally no one but Callie could see her. On the trail ride, though, when everyone had fallen, Melissa had twisted her ankle. Josh had gone for help, but before he could return, the first monsoon storm of the season had moved in. Somehow, Star had managed to make herself visible to all three girls then, so that Melissa could ride her to safety.

Star hadn't been visible to anyone else since that night. In a way, it really wasn't fair; Amy was helping keep Star secret, yet she couldn't even see the horse most of the time. But asking Star to appear when there wasn't an emergency didn't feel right somehow.

Someone else knocked on the door. "Come in," Callie said.

Her mom stepped into the room, brushing her damp red hair back from her shoulders. "Dinner's just about ready, Callie, assuming you can give us a hand setting the table."

"I thought it was Melissa's turn—" Callie began, but stopped at her mother's long look. "I'll be there in a minute, okay?"

"Okay," Mom said. She turned to Amy. "You're welcome to join us, of course."

"Thanks, Mrs. Fern," Amy said. "Josh is working late tonight, so that'd be great."

Callie looked out at the yard once more. Then she stood and followed Amy and Mom into the kitchen.

Much later that night, Callie lay awake in bed. The house was dark and silent, but Callie didn't plan to sleep, not yet. She hadn't even changed out of her clothes.

She planned to ride.

A breeze blew through her open window, carrying the scent of damp dust, though it still hadn't rained. An owl hooted across the yard. And then, without warning, an electric tingle ran down Callie's spine.

Callie smiled. "Star," she whispered. She climbed out of bed, walked to the window, and opened it. Her parents had finally replaced the rusty old screen that had come with the house. She pulled the new screen easily out of the frame and set it down on the floor. Her white plastic riding helmet sat on her dresser. Callie strapped it on. She'd gotten the helmet just a few days before. Her parents thought she'd wanted it only for her lessons; she'd told them she was tired of borrowing one of Sonoran Stables' helmets every time she rode there.

Not for the first time, Callie was glad her house was a single story. She climbed out the window, jumping easily to the ground on the other side, and looked out into the yard.

It seemed empty, but Callie knew better. She stood very still, waiting. No moon shone, and the sky was filled with more stars than she'd ever thought possible back when she lived in New York. The stars gave off faint light, as did the housing development on the other side of the wash.

Callie didn't know when she first saw it: a flicker like the swish of a tail, a twitch like the movement of an ear. The air wavered like water. For a moment she saw nothing more than a bright shadow. Then the world snapped into focus, a wet nose nudged at Callie's hand, and Star stood in front of her.

Callie used to think ghosts were misty and unreal, but Star was as solid as any horse, at least for Callie. Her silver-gray coat glimmered brightly, as if taking the starlight all around and reflecting it back toward the sky. The white star on her forehead shone, too, with a light all its own. Her mane fell graceful as foam down her long neck; on her back lay a smooth, worn leather saddle. Her tail swished impatiently back and forth, as if she wondered why Callie had taken so long to get there. Star was here because of Callie, after all. Even after all this time, Callie could barely believe it.

She threw her arms around Star's neck and hugged the horse tightly. The horse's hair was silky and soft against her cheek. She took a deep breath, inhaling Star's sweet cut-grass smell, so different from the horses she took lessons on.

As Callie held her, Star's ears perked happily about. She was thrilled to see Callie, as thrilled as Callie was to see her. Callie knew this, in the same corner of her mind where she somehow knew most of Star's emotions. Star knew Callie's feelings, too. That bond was one of the most amazing things about the horse.

Callie also knew Star wanted her to ride. She walked to Star's side, put her foot in the stirrup, and swung easily up onto the mare's back. As always, being on horseback felt wonderful. Callie looked around, enjoying how tall she was, feeling a warm breeze brush the back of her neck.

She froze at a sudden noise. Some small animal darted across Star's path, disappearing before Callie could tell what it was. Callie let out a breath. No one was there but she and Star. Not that she really needed to worry. Not only was Star invisible to other people, but when Callie rode, she was invisible, too.

Star stretched out her neck and sniffed at the ground, even though the creature was long gone. Then she turned her head around to look at Callie, through eyes that were dark and incredibly deep, and once more Callie felt the horse's eagerness to ride. She took Star's reins in her hand, though she didn't really need them, any more than she needed to kick Star to get her to go.

Walk, Callie thought.

Star started across the yard, her gait smooth and wonderfully light, as light as the breeze that still blew all around them.

Callie thought about riding in the corral, but that would mean thinking about the pool some more, and she didn't want to do that. She decided on the wash instead. Star, picking up on the thought, walked past the corral and the uprooted bushes.

Callie inhaled the smell of wet sand. Had it rained somewhere farther away? Beyond the wash, the mountains loomed, dark shadows against a slightly less dark sky. Something that sounded like a cricket chirped in the night air. A bird trilled once and was silent. Star stepped down into the sandy wash and started away from the house, picking her way carefully around the stones in her path. She seemed to see much better than Callie did at night. Could all horses see in the dark, or was it just because Star was a ghost?

At last they came to a spot where the light from the buildings on either side of the wash was much brighter than near Callie's house. Even Callie could see the ground beneath her clearly. She grinned.

Trot, she thought. Star broke into a bouncy two-beat gait.

Canter. Star sped into a three-beat lope, smoother, faster, and somehow much deeper than before.

Gallop. Star burst into a fiery four-beat run, kicking up sand as she ran. Star's lightness made Callie feel as though they were flying, as though at any moment they'd break free from the earth and never come back again. Wind brushed Callie's face and bare neck, caught in her throat. It blew Star's mane wildly around. Callie watched the houses race by, watched dark tree branches sway all around her. She laughed for joy.

As always, she lost track of how long she rode. The houses thinned out, and the wash grew dark again, but Star and Callie kept running.

Then all at once something—a tired, uneasy stirring at the back of Callie's mind—made Callie think, *Stop.* Star came to a crisp halt and turned to look at Callie. Callie looked back, into dark horse eyes.

Why had she thought that? She hadn't wanted to stop, not really. Had Star been the one who needed to turn around? For just a moment Callie had the feeling that Star was tired and wanted to go home. That didn't make any sense. Star never got tired, as far as Callie could tell. Still, Callie couldn't shake the idea that they should turn around. Maybe that was just because she knew she couldn't sleep late tomorrow, with school starting. She patted Star on the shoulder. "Let's go home."

They walked most of the way back. Callie dismounted by her window. As she turned to hug Star, she noticed something strange. Star's nose was running, as if she had a cold. Her eyes were watery, too; they glistened in the starlight.

"Are you okay?" Callie asked. Star merely nudged Callie's chest with her wet, runny nose. Callie smiled and scratched the horse behind the ears. "Well, you seem fine." She hugged Star again, then climbed back into her bedroom.

She felt Star's presence in her mind, even after she'd changed into pajamas and crawled into bed. She felt the horse's love for her, too, so solid and real that she thought if she opened her eyes she'd be able to see it. She had no idea how late it was, and she didn't look at her clock. Knowing would only make her more tired in the morning.

She fell asleep still aware of Star watching

her. After what seemed only minutes, she woke to a knock on her door.

"Callie!" Dad called. "Time to get up!"

Only half-awake, Callie stumbled out of bed to face her first day of school.

Chapter Two

Callie rubbed the grit out of her eyes, quickly showered, and got dressed, even though she wanted to crawl back into bed instead. She should have known better than to stay up so late. She'd had problems getting enough sleep because of Star before. Yet how could she not ride Star, whenever she had the chance? Callie still felt so lucky to have her back. And while Star showed up every night now, Callie never knew exactly when she would appear, and so she always feared that some night without warning Star wouldn't come at all.

By the time she went into the kitchen, she felt a little more awake. Dad stood by the stove, scrambling eggs. The smell of garlic and cinnamon filled the air. Dad's ideas about cooking were even weirder than Mom's sometimes.

Her mother sat hunched at the table, yawning over a cup of coffee. Both of Callie's parents were dressed for work: Mom for her job as a computer programmer, Dad for his job as an architect. Melissa sat next to her mother, an untouched plate of eggs in front of her. She wore a blouse and short skirt, high heels, and more makeup than Callie thought either of them was allowed. Callie hated thinking about clothes. She'd just pulled on jeans and a T-shirt for school; that always seemed safe enough. She'd rather have worn shorts, but she knew some schools didn't let kids wear them, and she didn't want to take any chances.

"I hate mornings," Melissa muttered as Callie slid into the seat beside her. Callie wasn't feeling too enthusiastic about the concept herself, at the moment.

Melissa tugged at her blouse, smoothed out some wrinkle in her skirt that Callie couldn't see. "You look fine," Callie said impatiently. Melissa didn't answer, just gave her sister one of the irritated looks Callie hated so much. Callie sighed. She got along with Melissa much better than she used to, but that didn't mean her sister didn't still drive her crazy sometimes. Melissa yawned, picked up a glass of juice, put it down again without drinking anything, and went back to looking over her outfit.

Only Dad seemed wide awake. He set a plate of eggs in front of Callie. "Amy stopped by while you were in the shower," he told her. "She said she won't be on the bus today. Josh always drives her in the first day, just like her parents used to. She's sorry she forgot to tell you."

Callie's stomach sank. It was bad enough she had to go to a school where she didn't know anyone. Now Amy wouldn't even be with her. She wished Amy could have somehow waited until the second day, when Callie knew her way around better, even though it was actually kind of neat that Josh was driving her in. Callie turned to her eggs without much enthusiasm. Dad and Mom hardly ever cooked breakfast; the first day of school was one of the few exceptions.

Ten minutes later, both of Callie's parents had driven off for work. They'd only come out to Tucson with one car, but now that they were settled into their jobs, they'd bought a second one. Callie and Melissa stood across the dirt road from their house, waiting for the bus; the stop was right in front of Amy's house. Josh's blue hatchback wasn't in the driveway, which meant he and Amy had already left.

The morning was already hot and damp; beneath Callie's backpack, her shirt clung to her skin. Her legs felt sticky in her jeans, too. She and Melissa stood together in silence. Melissa still kept adjusting her clothes; she also pulled a mirror out of her backpack to check her makeup. Melissa fussed like that a lot, but she seemed more nervous than usual today. Was she worried about starting a new school, too? As far as Callie could tell, Melissa never had trouble meeting people at school.

The high school Melissa was going to was farther away than Callie's middle school, so her sister's bus arrived first. The door opened, and Melissa started toward it.

"Good luck!" Callie called suddenly, not sure whether her sister really wanted or needed any luck from her.

Melissa glanced back at her. "Yeah," she said, with a faint smile, "you too." She disappeared into the bus without saying anything more.

Callie kept waiting. An iridescent green hummingbird darted just inches in front of her face, let out a squeaky chirp, and darted away again. She heard rumbling, looked down the street, and saw the bus, kicking up dust as it approached. She took a deep breath and glanced back at her house.

To her surprise, Star stood there watching, large eyes half hidden by a lock of silver-gray mane. Callie smiled. With Star seeing her off, her first day couldn't be all bad, could it?

Something was different about Star, but Callie couldn't figure out what. She seemed not to glisten quite as brightly, though that could have been because of the strong sun. Was her nose still running? In the bright light, it was hard to tell.

See you later. Callie wasn't sure Star could understand the exact words, but she felt the horse's enthusiasm at the thought. One ear perked forward. She snorted and started toward Callie, all full of silky grace, even at a walk. Before she could cross the road, though, the bus pulled up between them.

The door opened and Callie reluctantly got on. A blast of stuffy air hit her; like most buses, this one wasn't air-conditioned. When she looked out the window, Star was gone. She felt a sudden pang of loneliness. Did the loneliness come from her or Star? She couldn't tell.

She slid into an empty seat, though all she really wanted just then was to go back out and look for Star. Around her, other kids sat talking to one another in small groups, just like the kids on the bus at her old school had done. The difference now was that Callie didn't belong to any of these groups. That made her feel even lonelier.

"Are you new?" someone asked. Callie turned around to see a girl with blond hair and gold-rimmed glasses in the seat behind her.

Callie nodded, relieved to have someone to talk to. "I just moved here in June."

"Where are you from?" the girl asked.

A boy across the aisle from Callie broke in.

"Do you really need to ask?" He was slouched down in an oversized denim jacket, with dark eyes, straight black hair that fell well past his shoulders, and a voice that somehow made Callie feel as though he were laughing at her. "With that accent, she's got to be from New York. Right?"

The girl giggled. Callie's face turned hot. Her accent wasn't that strong, was it? Before she'd left Long Island, she hadn't even known she had one. Amy had commented on her sounding like a New Yorker once or twice, but she'd never made a big deal of it. "How can you tell, anyway?" Callie asked.

She must have still had an accent as she spoke, because the girl laughed again. Callie turned angrily away from her. If people laughed at her just for talking, how would she ever get through the day?

Across from her the boy said, "Hey, you have to admit you sound really weird." Callie glared out the window, trying to ignore him. "Besides, if you can't take a joke . . ." His voice trailed off.

The bus made a few more stops, then pulled into the school parking lot. Callie grabbed her backpack and hurried off with the other kids, though she wished she could go back home instead.

The building was one story instead of two,

but otherwise it looked pretty similar to any other school Callie knew. Above one set of doors a sign read CAÑADA DE LA PIRITA MIDDLE SCHOOL. The parking lot and sidewalks were filled with kids talking loudly, many more of them than at Callie's old elementary school. They wore everything from jeans and T-shirts to shorts, miniskirts, and halter tops.

Like on the bus, everyone here seemed to know someone else. Callie looked around for Amy, but didn't see her in the crowd. She felt like she had when she'd first moved to Tucson, as if she didn't quite belong. Star had helped her overcome her loneliness and fall in love with the city, but the horse couldn't help her when it came to meeting other kids. Callie drew her arms tightly around herself and walked inside.

The lobby was crammed with kids, too; their voices echoed off the walls, making the school seem even more crowded than it was. The building was cooler than the bus, but only barely; the air still felt heavy and warm. Someone brushed roughly past Callie, shoving her into a wall. "Hey!" Callie called, but the kid—whoever he was—had already disappeared into the crowd. Other kids pushed by, ignoring her completely.

At one end of the lobby, Callie found an office where a list of homerooms was posted. Her name was on the list, which at least meant she knew where she was supposed to go.

Or rather, she thought she did. The building had a lot more turns and corridors than Callie had expected. By the time she found the right classroom, the crowd had thinned out. She ran inside just as a bell rang, collapsing into the only seat she could find. Another kid entered a moment later, looked around, shrugged, and sat on the windowsill.

A woman with wavy brown hair and bright brown eyes stood at the front of the room. She introduced herself as Ms. Trujillo, their homeroom teacher, reached for a notebook on the desk beside her, and began calling out names.

Callie's name wasn't in the notebook.

"I'm sure it's not a problem." Ms. Trujillo's voice was cheerful and way too perky. "They always leave someone out the first day. Just tell me your name and I'll straighten things out later."

"Callie Fern." Callie winced, expecting more people to laugh at her accent, but no one did. Maybe that was just because the teacher was there. "I mean, Calliope Fern, but no one calls me that."

Ms. Trujillo smiled. "Well, it's good to have you here, Callie." She turned back to her notebook, pulled out a pile of papers with class schedules and locker numbers, and began passing them around. Someone from the office stopped by and handed Ms. Trujillo some more papers; Callie's schedule turned out to be in that stack.

As she walked around the room, Ms. Trujillo promised the kid on the windowsill that she'd get him a desk and chair by the next morning. "They're always one or two short on the first day," she explained cheerfully. With all the stuff they messed up the first day, Callie wished they'd just start a day later. Then she'd be home with Star now, instead of stuck here.

She sighed and looked over her schedule. Last year she'd gone to other rooms for a few classes, but this schedule had her running around all day. Just thinking about it made her tired.

"You can check out your lockers," Ms. Trujillo said, "and then go on to your first class." Callie picked up her backpack and followed everyone back into the hall.

Her lock stuck when she tried the combination. Wasn't anything going to go right? She tugged angrily at the lock, then tried the combination again. This time the lock clicked loose. Callie slammed the door open.

"Hey!" someone yelled. Callie looked around to see the boy from the bus, the one with the long hair and denim jacket. He had the locker next to hers, which meant he must have been in her homeroom, too. He rubbed the side of his nose, and Callie realized she'd hit him with her locker door.

She thought about apologizing, but then he looked at her, and something about his eyes, like his voice, made Callie feel as though he were laughing at her. "What's your problem?" he asked, glancing at the locker door as it swung loose on its hinges. He had a mild accent of his own, one Callie couldn't place. What had given him the right to say anything about Callie's accent, then?

"I'm not the one with problems," Callie snapped.

"I'm not the one with problems." The boy parroted the words back at her, in a deep, obnoxious voice she guessed was supposed to imitate her accent.

"Cut it out," Callie said. Why'd he have to be such a jerk?

The boy shook his head and said, back in his own voice, "You just watch it, okay?"

"Yeah, right," Callie said. Who did he think he was, to start telling her what to do? She pulled her lunch out of her backpack, threw it into her locker, and slammed the door shut. Without saying anything more, she slung the backpack over one shoulder and stormed off to find her first class.

By halfway through the day, Callie's backpack was full of books and she was exhausted. All of her classes seemed to be at opposite ends of the building; she'd been late for half of them.

Callie dumped the books into her locker—this time it opened without any trouble—pulled out her lunch, and followed everyone else to the cafeteria. The room, which smelled of old meatloaf, was crammed even more full of kids than the rest of the school. Callie wanted, more than anything, to be out in the desert instead of stuck inside all day. She looked around, wondering where to sit.

"Callie!" someone called. Callie saw Amy sitting at a table with a couple of other kids and waving at her. Callie was so relieved to see someone she knew. She crossed the room and slid into a seat across from her friend.

"So," Amy said, "you surviving middle school any better than the rest of us?"

Callie grimaced. "Barely." She pulled out her lunch. Since her parents had nothing to do with preparing it, the sandwich was just normal peanut butter and jelly.

"I know what you mean," Amy said. A tray with a plate of unidentifiable gray meat and some limp green vegetable sat in front of her. "All this running around sure is tiring, isn't it?" Amy turned to the two kids sitting with her. "Callie, this is Alicia and Matt."

Alicia popped the piece of gum she was

27

chewing, pushed some mystery meat around on her own plate, then asked, "Are you the new kid Amy keeps talking about?" She wore a sleeveless white blouse and had tight brown curls that just barely brushed her shoulders.

"I guess." Callie wondered what Amy had told them.

"So you really moved here all the way from New York?" Matt asked. He had orange, spiky hair, half hidden by a backward baseball cap. He tugged at the cap and took a bite of his tuna fish sandwich.

Callie sank deeper into her seat "How can everyone tell? Is my accent really that awful?"

"Well, you do have an accent," Matt admitted, "but I knew you were from New York mostly because Amy told me."

Alicia touched Callie's arm sympathetically. "When I moved here from Mexico, people were always telling me about my accent." She still had an accent now, but it was very faint. "Of course, the fact that I didn't speak English very well back then didn't help any."

"You're from Mexico?" Callie asked.

Alicia shrugged. "Tucson's only an hour from the border."

"I moved from Wisconsin myself," Matt said, "but I was way too young to remember."

"Is everyone here from somewhere else?"

Most of Callie's friends on Long Island had grown up there, just like she had.

Amy laughed. "Well, I was born here, you know. But this is sort of an immigrant city, for better or worse."

Callie looked around, wondering how many of the other kids were as new as she was. As she did, she saw the boy from the bus, walking across the cafeteria with a tray in his hands. He still wore his denim jacket, even though it was so warm inside. Callie scowled and turned back to the table.

"Ricky, over here!" Amy called. Callie looked up again to see Amy waving the boy over to them. Why would she want to do that?

"Callie, this is Ricky," Amy said as he approached. "He's another Arizona native." She grinned. "Though his relatives go back a lot further than mine. Anyway, we've known each other for about as long as I can remember."

Ricky smirked; the expression was gone before anyone else noticed. He set the tray down and slid into a seat. "We've already met," he said, giving her a long look. "Calliope from New York, right?"

Callie bristled. No one but her parents called her Calliope, and then only when she was in trouble. "It's Callie," she said through gritted teeth.

Ricky gave her another of his amused looks. "Callie from New York, then."

"Hey," Amy said, "Callie's the sort we want moving here, you know?"

"Sure she is." Ricky shrugged beneath his oversized jacket, making it clear he didn't agree.

Alicia leaned toward Callie. "Ricky and Amy have this thing about newcomers; they're always talking about whether or not people should move here." She popped her gum again. "The rest of us get pretty bored listening to them sometimes."

"But what's wrong with moving here?" Callie asked. She couldn't remember Amy going on about that when they'd first met. She'd complained a few times about some East Coast things—plants, mostly—not belonging in the desert, but that was all. Maybe she only talked about it around Ricky. Callie didn't see why anyone would want to talk about anything with Ricky, though.

Alicia shrugged. "Well, more people here means more crowds, more houses being built, more tearing up the desert, that sort of thing." Callie thought guiltily of the pool her dad was building. Did that count as tearing up the desert?

"But it also means meeting lots of cool people," Alicia said. She smiled. "I'm glad you're here, at any rate."

Callie smiled back. "Thanks."

Amy and Ricky were still talking, but their conversation had drifted to what they'd both been doing all summer. For the rest of lunch, Callie ignored Ricky as much as she could. Alicia and Matt seemed nice enough, though; Callie found herself getting to like them. Maybe school wouldn't be so bad after all.

The rest of the day went quickly enough. On the way home, Amy sat with Callie on the bus. As Ricky stepped on he glanced at Amy, then at Callie beside her. He walked past them, ignoring several empty rows to slouch down in a seat toward the back of the bus. Amy seemed puzzled at that; she watched him for a moment, then shrugged and turned back to Callie.

As the bus turned onto Callie's block, she heard Ricky's voice again. "Hey," he called out, "who's the idiot who let their horse get loose?"

Callie looked out the window, curious what horse he was talking about. Her jaw fell open. She couldn't believe what she saw.

The loose horse—the one Ricky had seen—was Star.

Chapter Three

Callie bolted to her feet. Around her, other kids began commenting on the "loose horse," too, even though none of them should have been able to see her.

What would people do if they found Star running around without a proper owner? Callie didn't want to find out. As soon as the bus door opened, she ran outside, Amy right behind her. She waited for the bus to leave, then ran up to Star and grabbed her reins. She started to pull Star around back, where at least fewer people would see her.

At first Star resisted, keeping her feet firmly planted on the ground, tail twitching stubbornly back and forth. Callie felt Star's confusion; she knew Star didn't understand what she was so worried about. Star nudged Callie curiously, her nose damp and warm against Callie's shirt. Callie reached up and stroked her silky neck.

Callie felt herself grow calmer. Staying upset was hard with Star around. She started toward the yard again, and this time Star followed. She dropped the reins, but Star kept walking beside her. Callie glanced back and saw hoofprints in the dirt. Star had only left hoofprints once before, the other time she'd been visible to people, up in the mountains.

"She's gorgeous," Amy said as they turned the corner into the yard. Callie had almost forgotten her friend was there.

Callie stopped walking once Star was safely hidden behind the house, glad her parents wouldn't be home for another couple of hours. She didn't want to think about how they'd react if they saw the mare. She was glad, too, that there were no workers today; Dad scheduled everyone to come by when he was home, so he could explain his plans in person.

Amy reached out a tentative hand to touch Star's neck, an awe-filled look crossing her face as she stroked the horse. Amy rode all the time with Josh down at Sonoran Stables, but she knew that Star was special, different from other horses. She ran her hand lightly along Star's mane, then turned to Callie and asked, "Do you think I could ride her? Just this once?" Amy had always wanted to ride Star, ever since she first learned about the ghost horse. Now that Star was visible, she probably could.

But Callie still wanted to know why people

could suddenly see Star. It didn't make any sense. "Something's wrong," she whispered. She took Star's head in her hands, stared deep into her dark eyes. "What is it?"

Star's nose was running, just as it had been last night; in her hurry to get Star out of sight, Callie hadn't noticed before. The horse's eyes were running, too. If that were all, Callie might not have been so worried, but the more she looked at Star, the more she could tell that other things were wrong, as well.

Star's coat was dull, more gray and less silver than usual. A lock of hair fell limply over her forehead. More than anything, Star looked tired—and she'd never looked tired before, not in all the nights that Callie had ridden her. Callie felt that tiredness, somewhere deep in her bones, as strongly as she felt her own after running around all day.

Amy must have noticed something was wrong, too, because all at once she asked, "Callie? Is Star sick?"

Callie's stomach tightened into a knot. "How can a ghost get sick?"

"I don't know." Amy shrugged uneasily. "But I do know a sick horse when I see one. For one thing, it's always a bad sign when their eyes start to run. Runny eyes are normal for humans, but not so common for horses."

Star nudged Callie's chest, once again picking up on Callie's concern. Callie turned to lean against her warm, silky shoulder. "What are you supposed to do when a horse gets sick?" Callie asked.

Amy bit her lip. "Usually you call the vet and ask what she thinks. That's what Josh did when he saw that Rusty was hurt, even though he has a pretty good idea of how to take care of injured or sick horses on his own by now. It never hurts to get another opinion, at least not when things look serious."

"But we can't call the vet," Callie said. Star snorted, as if in agreement—or maybe she was sneezing, Callie couldn't tell. She reached up and worriedly scratched Star behind the ears. Star stretched out her long neck, and Callie felt how much she enjoyed being scratched. Star turned her head around, looked at Callie, and snorted once more.

Amy nodded. "I know we can't call." She brushed a stray strand of hair out of her face; a breeze blew it back into her eyes again. The air was much drier than it had been that morning, and only a few wisps of clouds hovered over the mountains. "We have a bunch of horse medical books back home," Amy said. "Maybe there's something in them."

Callie took Star's head in her hands again, half hoping that if she stared at the horse long enough, she'd figure out what to do. As she stared, Star's ears began to shimmer brightly, so brightly that Callie could see right through them. The shimmering spread through the horse's head, out toward her mane. Callie caught her breath. She'd never seen Star begin to disappear, not while she was still with her. Star's jaw dissolved beneath Callie's hands, leaving her holding only shimmering air. Star's thoughts weakened, too, slowly fading out of Callie's mind.

"No!" Callie screamed. She had the sudden awful feeling that if Star disappeared now, she'd never see her again. Icy cold gripped her stomach. She threw her arms around Star's neck, terrified they would pass right through the horse, terrified Star would disappear forever.

Instead, Star turned solid and real in her arms. Callie held the mare tightly, breathing hard, afraid to ever let go. She pressed her cheek firmly against Star's warm neck, felt the horse's skin ripple beneath her as Star breathed.

Callie felt a human hand on her shoulder. "Are you okay?" Amy asked.

Callie took a deep breath and slowly stepped back from Star. The horse was still more gray than silver, but at least she was there again. She reached up and wound her fingers tightly into Star's mane.

"What happened? I mean, I saw Star begin

to fade, and then you yelled . . ." Amy's voice trailed off.

Callie explained as well as she could, one hand resting on Star's neck all the while.

Amy nodded seriously when Callie was through. "Do you think the way everyone can see Star, and the way she almost disappeared just now, are because of her being sick?"

Callie drew her arms around herself. "I don't know." Star went away every night, when they were done riding, but none of those other leavings had the same cold—the same *final*—feeling to them. It was as if Star could either be visible to everyone now or gone completely, but nothing in between.

What if the next time Star started to disappear, Callie wasn't there to stop her?

Beyond the house, Callie heard the sound of a car along the dirt road. Were Mom and Dad home already? It seemed too early.

"That's probably Josh," Amy said. "He's working a short shift today. He'll want to know how school was. And I want to check how Rusty's doing; the vet was supposed to see him today." Amy hesitated, as if reluctant to leave her friend. "How about I come by later tonight with some of those horse books? Maybe we can figure something out."

Callie nodded. "That'd be great."

Amy patted Star on the shoulder. Then she

turned and ran around the house to meet Josh, backpack swinging over one shoulder.

Callie sighed and leaned back against Star. "I wish you could just tell me what's wrong," she said. But for all Star's magic, the one thing she couldn't do was talk directly to Callie, any more than other horses could. Michael, the ghost of Star's original owner, had talked to her once, but that was weeks ago, and there had barely been time to ask him anything before he disappeared again. Callie had no idea whether he'd ever return.

Star stretched her neck around to lean her head on Callie's shoulder, as if trusting Callie to fix the problem, whatever it was. Their long shadows stretched across the yard. What time was it? Her parents would be home soon. "How am I going to keep Mom and Dad from seeing you?" Callie wondered aloud.

"You could let me take care of that."

Callie looked up, startled. Melissa stood just a few feet away, near Star's corral, holding a tape measure one of the workers must have left behind. How long had she been there? Callie hadn't even seen her enter the yard, or heard the bus drop her off.

"You're so funny when you're around horses," Melissa said. "You hardly notice anything else. If you really want to keep Star hidden, you ought to be more careful."

"I am being careful," Callie snapped, annoyed at the tone in Melissa's voice—like she was older and superior, somehow.

Melissa didn't seem to notice. "Anyway, I can keep Mom and Dad out of the way tonight, if you want," she said. "Until you can figure out a better way to hide Star."

Callie looked up at Melissa, startled by—and grateful for—the offer of help. "Thanks," Callie said. "Thanks a lot."

Melissa shrugged. "Well, I owe Star one, you know. I would have been stranded without her." All at once she looked embarrassed. Callie hadn't wanted to tell Melissa about Star, but her sister had kept the secret well. That was one of the reasons Callie liked her a lot more than she used to.

"Anyway, I thought Star was supposed to be invisible," Melissa said.

"She was," Callie told her, but before she could explain she heard another car, and this time it really was one of their parents pulling into the driveway. Melissa glanced at Star, then went around front without saying anything else. Callie stayed with Star a few seconds more, then followed.

Melissa did as she'd promised, distracting their mother and father through the evening. She rambled on about high school, about the other kids, about some guy named Todd she'd met in math class. When Dad mentioned going out into the yard to check on a few things—as an architect, he was always making small changes to his plans for the pool—Melissa asked him to help with her algebra homework instead.

Not long after dinner, Amy showed up with an armload of books, saying she and Callie had some homework of their own. Callie's mom and dad were both impressed by that; usually she put off her homework as long as she could. What they didn't know was that she was putting it off now, too, since all of Amy's books were horse books.

Callie and Amy went into her bedroom. Callie pulled the door shut behind them, and Amy dumped the books down on the floor. The pile was huge; Callie wondered just how many medical horse books Amy and Josh had. Then again, she'd been inside Amy's house. Amy's bedroom was filled with bookshelves, and there were shelves in most of the other rooms, too, with books on all sorts of subjects. Amy read anything she could get her hands on. In her house that was quite a bit.

"How's Rusty?" Callie asked her friend.

"The vet never made it over; she had an emergency colic case on the other side of town. She said she'll be by tomorrow—unless there's another emergency." Amy sighed, sprawled out on the carpet, and started skimming through a book. Callie chose another book and did the same. The book fell open to a section on leg injuries. Had Josh been going through those pages after Rusty was hurt? She flipped forward, looking for information that had more to do with Star.

Through the window, she saw Star down near the wash, nosing around a small cluster of trees. Hoofprints led across the yard; Callie hoped no one would notice. The sun had set a while ago, and only the last gray of twilight remained.

As Callie read, she grew discouraged. Hundreds of things could make a horse tired and cause her nose and eyes to run, everything from eye infections to horse versions of flu, pneumonia, and strep throat. The majority of the diseases weren't very serious—most of the time. Practically all of them were fatal some of the time. And all of the treatments seemed to involve changing the horse's food or having a vet prescribe medicine, which meant they weren't any use to Star, who, as far as Callie could tell, never ate anything.

"At least ghosts can't die," Amy said. She meant to be comforting, but Callie thought of the icy cold feeling she'd gotten when Star had almost disappeared. Maybe instead of dying, ghosts just disappeared and never came back.

Callie set her book aside and opened another, but she couldn't focus on it. She thought about the other dangers she and Star had faced together. They'd been through the monsoon in the mountains, but the rain hadn't touched Star. They'd been through a fire together, too, but the flames had turned out to be ghost flames, and Star hadn't been hurt by them, either.

"Ghost germs?" Callie said aloud. "Is that what's hurting Star?"

Amy giggled. Callie looked sharply over at her. "How can you laugh?"

"It does sound funny," Amy told her. "I can just picture these little germs, with little ghostly white sheets over their heads—" She laughed louder.

The image *was* funny. Callie started laughing, too, then stopped herself. "This is serious," she said.

Amy's face turned sober. "But it's exactly when serious things happen that you need to laugh. You'll go crazy otherwise. Trust me, I know." Amy looked straight at Callie, and the intensity of her gaze made Callie uncomfortable. Amy knew about serious stuff happening. Callie couldn't think of anything worse than having both your parents die at once, without warning. Had Amy really been able to laugh then? Callie couldn't bring herself to ask.

A grin crossed Amy's face, breaking up the serious look completely. "Ghost germs," she repeated. "Ghost bugs. Ghost bacteria. Ghost—" She burst into giggles once more. Callie started giggling, as well, and this time she didn't try to stop herself. Laughing felt good, so good that Callie laughed harder.

All at once she felt Star's presence nudging at her mind; she looked up and saw the horse standing with her damp nose right up against the window. She must have crossed the yard while Callie was laughing. The sky was dark now, and behind Star a half moon cast pale silver light across the yard. The light reflected off Star's coat, making her shine in the night like a glowing shadow. Callie smiled. Then a wispy cloud moved across the moon and the light faded, leaving Star gray and tired-looking once more.

Star nudged at the screen. Callie felt the mare's restless thoughts, urging her to climb outside. *Later*, Callie promised. Star stared at Callie through watery eyes, until Callie wasn't sure she could bear to just stay in the house and watch her. But then Star turned away and started slowly back across the yard.

More than anything, Callie wanted to ride when she went outside, but one thing the books made clear was that you shouldn't ride a sick horse. "How am I going to explain not riding to Star?" Callie wondered aloud.

"Well, you could at least walk her around," Amy said. "Sometimes that can help work an illness out of a horse's system." She slammed shut the book she was reading and reached for another, glancing at the clock as she did. Callie followed her gaze; it was nearly ten. "I'd better get going," Amy said. She started gathering up the books all around them.

Callie walked Amy outside. With the sun down, the air was merely warm, not hot like during the day. "Lots of horse problems go away on their own," Amy said. "Maybe that'll happen with Star, too."

"I hope so," Callie told her.

Amy shifted from one foot to the other. "If there's anything I can do to help, just let me know, okay? I'll keep reading and thinking about other possible cures."

"Thanks," Callie said. "Thanks a lot."

Amy shrugged. "I'd do just about anything to help Star. Star and you both." She turned and walked across the street without another word.

When Callie got back inside, most of the lights were turned out. Down the hall she heard her family moving around, getting ready for bed. She locked the front door behind her and went into her own room. Still dressed, she turned off the lights and crawled under the covers. Tonight, even more than most nights, she wasn't planning to sleep. Not with Star still out there, still sick, needing her.

Mom knocked and opened the door. " 'Night, Callie,'' she said. "See you in the morning.''

" 'Night, Mom.'' Callie waited while she closed the door.

She felt Star's eager presence, somewhere outside, and knew that Star wanted to be with her, too. She glanced at the window. Star stood there again, nose against the screen. The moon had disappeared behind the other side of the house, and in the faint starlight, Star was little more than a gray shadow. Callie swallowed. It was bad enough that Star looked so gray during the day. She'd always shone more brightly at night.

Callie sat up, wrapping her arms around her knees, and waited for her family to sleep.

Chapter Four

Eventually Callie's family stopped moving around. When Callie poked her head out the bedroom door, she heard only their slow, regular breathing, and she knew they were asleep.

She crawled out the window, into a night no longer quite so warm. Star stood waiting for her. Callie hugged the horse tightly. Star shifted impatiently, and Callie knew she wanted, more than anything, to ride. Callie touched Star's face near the horse's eyes; her hand came away damp and sticky. The moon had completely set, and in the dim light Star was still more gray than silver. Only her wet eyes glimmered in the darkness.

"I can't ride," Callie said, though she longed to swing up onto Star's back. Instead, she took Star's reins to lead her around. Star seemed confused by that at first, but then she snorted— the sound was like a shrug—and followed Callie. Callie led the horse to the corral and walked her around in large circles. After a few steps she released the reins, draping them over

Star's neck, but Star kept following as if Callie were holding them anyway.

After a while, Star quickened her pace. Callie walked faster to keep up. Star broke into a trot, and Callie ran to stay abreast of her. When Star began to canter, Callie couldn't run fast enough. So she went to the center of the ring, where just by turning in circles she could see Star run. She watched, breathless, as Star's powerful legs hit the ground in three-beat rhythm, watched her mane and tail flow gracefully out behind her, a gray shadow racing through the night. Star burst from a canter into a gallop and kept running.

Callie didn't know when Star started to tire out, but all at once the mare's gallop was awkward and uneven. Star began breathing hard, sweat dripping down her sides, even though she'd never sweated at all before. She slowed to a walk, then stopped completely. Callie ran to her. Star looked up, and Callie felt a wave of exhaustion. By running like that, Star had completely worn herself out.

Callie should have known that if Star was too sick to ride, she'd be too sick to run, too. But Star had wanted to run so badly. She'd be fine once she rested, wouldn't she? Callie swallowed. She had to be okay.

Callie couldn't leave Star alone now, not when the mare felt so awful. She draped an arm over Star's sweaty neck and stood with her. Something slithered by Callie's and Star's feet. Instead of tensing up, Star barely noticed. Callie sighed and leaned closer against the horse.

She didn't expect to fall asleep standing there like that, but she did. When she woke, the world was shrouded in pale dawn light. Her arm felt cold. She stretched, lifted the arm stiffly from Star's neck, and glanced at it. What she saw made the cold seem to spread to the rest of her body. Callie stared and stared, unable to believe it.

Her hand shimmered silver in the morning light. Callie saw the ground right through it. Trembling, she touched her hand to her cheek. Her hand passed through, as if it didn't exist at all. As Callie watched, the shimmering spread up her arm, all the way to her elbow. She glanced at Star, and saw that Star shimmered, too, just as she had yesterday, when she'd almost disappeared.

Panic caught at the back of Callie's throat. She stared numbly at her hand, not knowing what to do, not able to stop staring. Her arm couldn't be disappearing like that, not really. She shook her arm, hard, desperate to make the shimmering stop.

"Callie?" someone called. Callie recognized Dad, calling from her bedroom. Something about his voice made the cold feeling in Callie's hand recede a little. Dad called again—he sounded a little bit angry—and the feeling disappeared completely. As Callie watched, her hand and arm turned solid once more. She touched her face. Hand met cheek as if that were the most natural thing in the world. Beside Callie, Star looked solid, too. Callie took one deep breath, then another, trying to convince herself she really was all right.

Dad called a third time, and Callie knew he would come out into the yard if she didn't answer him. If he did, he'd see Star. *You'd better hide*, Callie thought, hoping Star would understand. Star seemed to; she reluctantly turned and walked away, toward some trees where she wouldn't easily be seen. Callie felt her tiredness as she walked.

"I'm here!" Callie called out. She ran to the house.

Her father stood by her open window, one hand holding the screen she'd left on the floor. "What are you doing up so early?" he asked. "And why is your screen out?"

Callie swallowed. "I couldn't sleep," she said quickly. "I decided to go for a walk. And I—I didn't want to wake anyone up by walking through the rest of the house."

Dad looked at her suspiciously, and Callie

knew he wasn't sure whether to believe her. Outside, the gray light had given way to the pink of early morning. "Well, just get in here and get ready for school," he said at last.

Callie nodded and started to climb in the window. Dad stopped her. "The other way, Callie." Callie started around the house, while her father put the screen back into the frame.

In the shower, Callie stared down at her hand again, watching streams of water flow over the now-solid skin. What exactly had happened out in the yard? Would she really have disappeared if Dad hadn't called? Was Star's strange ghostly illness somehow contagious? Callie shivered as she stepped out of the shower, pulling a towel tightly around her.

Ghost germs, she thought. Suddenly the idea didn't seem very funny at all.

Chapter Five

Callie got dressed—wearing shorts instead of jeans this time—and went out to the kitchen. She wanted to check on Star again before school, but she was afraid Dad would get suspicious if she went into the yard a second time. Instead, she mumbled a few words to her family, poured herself a bowl of cereal, and sat yawning at the table as she ate it. How long had she actually slept last night? It couldn't have been much, standing up like that.

Finally she and Melissa headed out the door, their parents right behind them. "Don't forget your riding lesson after school," Mom said as she got into her car.

Melissa laughed. "Like Callie ever forgets anything to do with horses."

Callie scowled at Melissa; Melissa rolled her eyes. Their mom just looked at them both, but before she could say anything, Callie started across the street. She was grateful her parents were letting her take lessons at all. After everyone had been thrown on the last trail ride,

51

Mom and Dad had wanted Callie to give up horses completely; only with Melissa's help had she changed their minds. Callie had just gone back to her lessons a week ago. Melissa had had her first riding lesson then, too, which had gone surprisingly well—much better than any of her trail rides, at any rate.

Amy was already at the bus stop. Callie walked over to her. The morning was hot and dry, the sky deep blue and cloudless.

"How's Star?" Amy asked at once. Callie explained how quickly Star had gotten tired while she was running last night, but before she could tell Amy about falling asleep and waking up with her hand all strange, Melissa joined them.

Melissa listened to Callie and Amy for a moment, then asked, "Are you forgetting to sleep because of Star *again*? Didn't you learn anything the last time?"

"I didn't *forget* to sleep," Callie snapped. "But Star's sick. She needs me out there."

"Why?" Melissa asked, sounding genuinely puzzled.

"What do you mean, 'why'?"

"Well, Star's a ghost, right?" Melissa said. Callie nodded. "So it's not like anything that happens to her matters—not really. She's already dead."

"Of course it matters!" Callie said. And not

just because she'd miss Star terribly if anything happened to her, either. Star might be dead, but that didn't make her any less real. Some important part of her still existed; all the thoughts of Star's that Callie felt were proof of that. Was it right to say her soul was still alive? Maybe, but that sounded kind of stupid, so Callie didn't say anything to Melissa.

Melissa's bus pulled up in front of them. "Well, try to get some sleep tonight, okay?" Melissa's voice still had an edge Callie hated, but behind it, she had to admit she could hear concern. Melissa got onto the bus without saying anything more.

Callie and Amy's bus arrived soon after. Callie yawned as she got on. She glanced out the window. She didn't see Star outside, but she felt something—a pang of loneliness so sharp that she nearly burst into tears. She swallowed. There was no way Callie could explain to Star about school, or why she needed to go away so often now. *Stay hidden*, Callie thought, hoping Star would understand. Then she slid into a seat. Amy sat down beside her.

Ricky was sitting across from them again, slouching in his denim jacket. Ignoring Callie, he looked at Amy and asked, "Did you ever find out where that horse came from yesterday?"

Amy shifted uneasily. "Just someone down

the road who'd left their gate open. They showed up after the bus left."

"But no one on your street owns any horses," Ricky said. "Not unless someone moved in while I was gone this summer."

Amy looked down, avoiding Ricky's gaze. Callie could tell Amy was uncomfortable lying to Ricky—almost as much as she was lying to Josh. It made Callie uncomfortable, too. She wished Ricky would stop asking questions.

"The owners live the next block over," Amy said, still not looking at Ricky. "Some new people."

"Just what we need." Ricky cast a sidelong look at Callie, then turned back to Amy. "Well, I hope that horse is okay, with its owners just letting it get out like that."

Amy and Callie exchanged glances. "Me too," Amy said.

"Do you think maybe you should tell Josh about it?" Ricky asked.

"No!" Amy blurted out, her voice a strangled yelp. At Ricky's startled expression, she lowered her voice and said, "I mean, I already spoke to him, and he said he thought everything was okay."

Ricky gave Amy a strange look, as if he weren't quite convinced, but he didn't ask anything more. For the rest of the ride, he kept glancing at them both, as if wondering what was really going on. Finally the bus pulled into the school lot. Callie stood and stepped into the aisle, yawning some more as she did.

Behind her, Ricky said, "Are these long bus rides too much for you, Callie from New York?"

"What's it to you?" Callie asked. Ricky just smirked and pushed past her off the bus.

"Jerk," Callie muttered under her breath. She stepped outside, Amy beside her.

"Hey," Amy said quietly. "Ricky's not a jerk."

"Then why's he always so obnoxious to me?" Callie demanded, not nearly so quietly.

Amy didn't answer. "I don't like it when people insult my friends," she said instead. "I don't like hearing Ricky talk like that about you, either."

"What do you mean?" Callie turned to face Amy, her face growing hot. "What did Ricky say about me?"

Amy sighed, sounding a little tired herself. "I wish you would both stop, really."

"I never started anything," Callie protested. "He did. Just because he can't stand anyone new. How does he make any friends at all that way?"

"Some of the new people who move here really are pretty annoying," Amy said impatiently. Callie wondered whose side she was on. "You get the feeling they don't really care about the desert at all, that they want to pull it apart and change it into something else. They're so busy digging things up, putting in housing developments, wasting too much water just so they can grow plants that don't belong here—if you watch that sort of stuff long enough, you get kind of tired of it, you know? And easterners can be so loud and pushy—"

"But I'm not like that!" Callie said, tired of listening to Amy go on. Her voice came out louder than she expected. Without warning, Amy giggled.

"What's so funny?" Callie demanded.

"Not loud at all," Amy said, stifling another giggle.

Callie wanted to say that wasn't funny, but then she realized it was, really. A smile tugged at her face. Amy laughed louder. As always, Amy's laughter was contagious; soon Callie was laughing, too. Some kid turned to stare at them, but Callie didn't care. Around her, the crowd began to thin out. From inside the school, a bell rang.

"Come on," Amy said, still grinning. "We'll be late." Callie followed her friend inside.

As she did, she couldn't help thinking about Ricky. That cut her laughter short, made her angry all over again. What right did he have to talk about her behind her back, to the one real friend she had here? She hoped Amy wouldn't take anything he told her seriously.

"Ricky is right about one thing," Amy said, as if reading Callie's thoughts.

Callie stiffened. "What's that?"

"You do look awfully tired. Are you going to stay out with Star tonight, too?"

"I have to," Callie said. "I feel bad enough being gone all day today." She remembered the loneliness she'd felt as the bus had driven off. Besides, the more time she spent with Star, the more time she had to figure out what was wrong. And she was still afraid Star would disappear and not come back while she was away.

"I know." Amy nodded solemnly, all traces of laughter gone from her face. "That's why I want to help. I don't think Josh will notice if I'm gone for just a few hours tonight. If I watch Star for a little while, you can get some sleep."

Callie hesitated. She'd never left anyone else alone with Star. Then again, no one had been able to see the horse until now. If she was going to trust anyone, it would be Amy.

Amy knew a lot more about horses than Callie did. Maybe she'd figure out what was really wrong.

"All right." Callie hesitated a moment more. "Thanks," she said. "Thanks a lot."

Another bell rang. Neither Callie nor Amy said anything more after that; they were too busy running the rest of the way to their classes.

Today Ms. Trujillo knew Callie's name, at least, and had enough chairs for everyone. Callie found her way around the school more easily, too, in spite of how tired she was. But in history class she discovered that, by spending the whole night reading horse books, she'd completely forgotten that she had history homework. Callie promised to turn it in by the end of the day; the teacher, a gray-haired man named Mr. Johnson, seemed to accept that easily enough.

After history she had lunch. She found Amy, Matt, Alicia, and Ricky already in the cafeteria. Callie said hello to everyone except Ricky. She slid into a seat, opened her lunch, pulled her history book from her backpack, and started reading.

Matt glanced over her shoulder. "Assignment for Johnson?" he asked. Callie nodded. Matt took a bite out of his sandwich. "Couple of my older brothers had him. They say he's a nice guy and all, but he sure gives a lot of work sometimes."

"I can tell." Callie grimaced as she kept reading. What kind of a teacher gave homework on the first day, anyway?

She turned to the questions at the back of

the chapter. The questions asked about different people who'd settled in Arizona at different times. Callie really must be tired; she could barely remember what she'd just read. There'd been English and Spanish settlers, but before that there'd been a whole bunch of different Native American tribes, too. Callie flipped back through the pages. She wasn't even sure how to pronounce most of the names, let alone tell them all apart. She turned to Matt, who was still looking over her shoulder. "What's the difference between the Yaqui, Apache, and Tohono O'odham, anyway? They all lived here, right?"

Ricky snickered. Callie looked sharply up. She hadn't even been talking to him. "Everyone knows that those Indians are all alike," he said.

Callie was getting so tired of him. "What would you know about it, anyway?" she asked.

Ricky gave her a long, sarcastic look. "As a member of the White Mountain Apache tribe, I think I know quite a bit."

Callie's cheeks turned red. "Well, I didn't know."

"Of course not." All at once Ricky sounded as if he were laughing at her again. "Just what did you expect an Indian to look like, Callie from New York?"

"I wish you'd stop calling me that," Callie told him.

"I'm sure you do," Ricky said.

Callie turned angrily back to her notebook, not talking to anyone at all for the rest of lunch. She finished her homework in silence and turned it in to Mr. Johnson at the end of the day, just as she'd promised.

She expected—and worried—that Star would be waiting out front after school again, where everyone could see her, but she wasn't. Callie stepped off the bus, Amy close behind. To her surprise, Ricky followed them both.

"What do you want now?" Callie asked. She wished he would leave her alone already.

Ricky glared at her. "I only live about a mile away, you know."

"I don't remember seeing you around this summer," Callie said suspiciously.

Ricky shrugged. "I spent some time visiting family up north, and then I went out to New Mexico with my parents, who were doing some research there."

"Ricky's dad is with the geology department over at the university," Amy explained. "My mom used to work on campus, too; it's how our families first met."

"Well, this still isn't your stop," Callie snapped. She didn't want Ricky hanging around in front of her house, especially not when Star could show up at any moment.

"So I feel like walking," Ricky said. "And I want to check out where that loose horse we saw yesterday lives. Make sure your out-of-town neighbors had the sense to keep their gate shut today."

Amy bit her lower lip, but didn't say anything. Ricky glanced at them both a moment, then turned away, starting down the dirt road without another word.

Callie sighed. "Why does he care, anyway?" She kept her voice low enough that Ricky couldn't hear.

"He's probably just curious," Amy said. "Wouldn't you be?"

"Well, I hope he's not *too* curious," Callie said. The last thing she needed was for Ricky to start wondering about Star.

She expected Amy to defend Ricky again, but Amy only said, "Me too. It's hard enough trying to keep Josh from finding out about her." She looked at Callie, as if expecting some answer to that, but Callie had no idea what to say. They waited in silence for Ricky to disappear around a corner, then went into the backyard. Star wasn't there, either.

"Star?" Callie called. She had a sudden image of the mare standing among some mesquite trees, sniffing at a bright green bush, her gray coat deep and rich beneath a brilliant blue sky. Callie didn't know exactly where Star was, only that she'd never been there herself. Star must have understood when Callie said to stay hidden that morning.

As Callie watched, Star looked up and stared straight at her, as if somehow, through the vision, the mare saw her perfectly. Star turned away from the trees and started walking in some direction Callie assumed was toward home. She walked faster, then broke into a trot.

No, Callie thought. *Walk. I'll wait.* She felt Star's reluctance as the horse slowed down. Star was already breathing hard, but she wanted to keep running, both for the joy of it and to reach Callie as fast as she could. Callie didn't want Star wearing herself out again, though.

The vision dissolved. As it did, Callie realized just how hot it was outside. The sun was a huge yellow ball above the house. Wind blew dust across the yard.

"Star's on the way," Callie said. Amy nodded. "Want something to drink?" Callie asked.

"Sure," Amy said.

They went inside. As she poured two glasses of juice, Callie's thoughts wandered from Star back to Ricky. She wondered again why he cared about Star. She kind of felt as though he'd tricked her into making a fool of herself at lunch, too. "Why didn't Ricky just say he

was Apache when I first met him?" Callie
asked.

"Why would he?" Amy asked, seeming startled by the question. At Callie's puzzled look
she asked, more quietly, "Do you tell everyone
you meet where you're from right away?"

"I guess not," Callie admitted. She sighed.
"They all tell me instead."

"Oh, your accent'll fade soon enough," Amy
told her.

"Is it . . ." Callie hesitated, afraid her question would sound stupid. "Do you think it's
because Ricky's relatives were here first that
he hates new people so much?"

"Stop worrying about it," Amy said, as if she
were tired of Callie bringing up the subject.
Callie handed a glass to Amy; they both
stepped out onto the screened patio. Wind had
blown dust through the screen, covering the
chairs with a thin layer of grit.

"You know," Amy said, blowing dust off one
of the chairs, "the Apache weren't the first people here. They came from way up north origi-
nally. I'm sure the Tohono O'odham weren't
too thrilled when they showed up. And back
before the O'odham there were the Hohokam,
who seem to have disappeared completely."

Callie sat down and took a long drink of
juice. She wondered whether anyone got anywhere, really, without making things more

crowded or shoving other people out of the way. She wondered where she fit in, having only just moved there that summer.

She took another drink, stopping when she felt a familiar presence in her mind. She stepped outside the patio and saw Star standing behind the house, tail swishing back and forth, eyes intent on Callie, sweaty coat glistening beneath the hot sun. Callie set her glass down and ran around back. Star's ears perked forward. Callie hugged the horse.

She felt Star's enthusiasm at seeing her, but also something else—the same terrible loneliness she'd felt earlier that day. "But I'm here now," Callie said. She hugged Star tighter, inhaling a mouthful of dust as she did. Callie coughed. She stepped back to take a better look at the horse.

Star looked even sicker than she had that morning.

Her head drooped wearily toward the ground; her mane was dirty and tangled against her neck. Her coat was matted with dirt and sweat, and she looked really tired—like a normal horse who'd been out on the trail all day, only worse. Dirt had never touched Star before, any more than rain or sweat had. Now she looked like she needed a bath and good grooming. Callie swallowed. How much sicker could Star get, before Callie somehow lost her forever? She didn't know, didn't want to know. Just thinking about it made her want to cry.

Star looked up at Callie, through eyes that were watery, but still incredibly deep, and it was as if she were looking straight inside Callie, reading the thoughts she found there. Callie felt a wave of love and comfort from the horse. Star might be sick herself, but that wasn't enough to keep her from caring when Callie got upset.

"Are you okay?" Amy touched Callie's shoulder.

"Yeah." Callie swallowed again, ran a hand through Star's tangled mane. "What's *wrong*?" she asked. She stared at Star hard, willing Star to understand the question and to tell her, through images or thoughts or something, what to do about it.

Instead, Star started shimmering. The cold feeling that meant Star might leave gripped Callie once more. "No!" Callie screamed. She threw herself at the horse. Star felt solid enough beneath her, but when Callie looked down at her own arms, they were shimmering, too. This time the shimmering quickly spread to the rest of her body, until she could see right through herself. Every part of her felt cold, in spite of the hot desert sun. She started shivering and couldn't stop.

"Callie?" Amy called. Her voice sounded

thin and very far away. Callie turned to face her friend. What she saw made her shiver even harder.

Amy wavered in front of Callie, as if she stood on the other side of a thick wall of water. Around Amy, the yard was very faint, like a faded old painting. And beyond the edges of the yard, Callie saw a swirling grayness like nothing she'd ever seen before. It looked a little like mist, only thicker and more dangerous. As she watched, tendrils of gray crept forward, from all directions at once. The tendrils thickened, until they almost looked like human fingers, attached to human hands, reaching toward her.

Amy stepped forward. Her movements seemed slow, unreal. She reached out a hand to Callie. Callie reached back, and their hands went right through each other. The color drained from Amy's face, and that made her look even less real, more a part of the faded yard she stood in.

"So, anyway," a voice said cheerfully, "this is where I live." It was Melissa's voice, coming from somewhere in front of the house. She sounded so normal. The gray tendrils seemed to back away in response.

"Want me to show you around inside?" Melissa asked someone. The grayness thinned, like mist broken up by sunlight. The tendrils recoiled further, then all at once dissolved.

When Callie looked down at herself, she was solid once more. Star was solid, too. A hot wind blew, and Callie stretched out her arms, for once grateful for the burning air against her skin. She let out her breath.

Amy walked slowly up to Callie. Her face was still pale. "What happened?"

"I don't know." Callie explained, as well as she could, what had gone on.

Amy took a deep breath. "How weird. From here it looked like you were fading, like all the color had washed itself out of you and you were disappearing. You and Star both. And then I tried to touch you, and I couldn't. You were hardly there at all."

Callie was still shaking. Star, picking up on her distress, moved closer to her. Callie leaned against the horse. Star's warmth was reassuring.

Amy bit her lip. "What do you think would have happened," she asked suddenly, "if you and Star had faded all the way?" She almost sounded more curious than frightened. "Would you have wound up in that strange gray place? Do you think those weird gray hands actually belonged to anyone, to other ghosts maybe?"

"I don't know." Callie drew her arms around herself. "I don't want to know."

Amy's face took on a strange, serious look. "I do," she whispered. Or maybe Callie had heard wrong. She couldn't imagine why anyone would want to bring that awful grayness back. A moment later the look disappeared, and Amy said, almost too lightly, "My throat's parched. Let's go inside and get something to drink."

Callie couldn't believe Amy was even suggesting she leave Star now, after what had just happened. Amy started toward the house, though, and as she did, Callie realized she really was thirsty again. In the heat, with the air so dry, her throat was rough and scratchy. It was amazing how fast you could dehydrate in the desert.

Callie hesitated, then patted Star on the shoulder. "I'll be back soon," she promised. Still wondering if she'd heard Amy right, she followed her friend toward the patio.

Halfway there she stopped and glanced back at Star. The horse looked perfectly solid, and there was no hint of swirling gray mist anywhere.

She wished she knew how to make sure that things stayed that way.

Chapter Six

Amy and Callie filled their glasses with water this time, sat down on the kitchen chairs, and drank them down. Melissa stepped into the room, followed by a boy with short blond hair and bright green eyes. "Hi, guys," she said, smiling broadly. She reached out and took the boy's hand in her own. "Todd, this is my sister, Callie. And this is Amy—the one whose brother works with horses."

"Hi," Todd said. "Melissa told me about that horseback ride you guys went on." Callie stiffened, wondering how much Melissa had actually told Todd, but he only said, "I think you were all pretty brave, after getting thrown like that, to spend the whole night in the mountains."

Callie shrugged. She hadn't felt very brave at the time, but Melissa's idea of bravery was different from Callie's, anyway. Or maybe she was just trying to impress Todd.

Melissa tugged on Todd's hand. "Come on," she said. "I'll show you the backyard. It's huge, and my parents are putting in a pool."

Callie tensed. Star was still in the yard. "Um, maybe you don't want to go out quite yet," she said.

"Of course we do," Melissa said. She glanced at Callie, and Callie looked back, hoping Melissa would understand why she couldn't go out there. Melissa rolled her eyes, but to Todd she said, "Let's go out front first. The patio's always all dusty, anyway." Everything was dusty in Tucson, but Todd didn't argue with her excuse. Callie watched as Melissa turned and led Todd back through the living room.

Callie wouldn't be able to keep Todd out of the backyard forever. *You need to hide*, she thought. She felt Star's disappointment and loneliness, but she also had an image of the horse slowly walking away. Callie sighed. It was so hard to send Star off like that, yet as long as other people could see the horse, she couldn't risk anyone else discovering her.

Even with Star trying to stay hidden, how long could Callie really keep everyone from discovering the mare? She hoped Star got better before she found out.

The front door slammed shut behind Melissa and Todd. Amy started giggling.

"What's so funny now?" Callie asked.

"Two days," Amy said.

"Two days for what?"

"Two days for your sister to get a boyfriend. I was betting on a week, at least."

Callie smiled. "You didn't know Melissa back in New York. I'm amazed she waited this long." At least Melissa was finally meeting other kids, though. She'd been pretty lonely over the summer, without anyone her age to talk to.

Callie glanced out the kitchen window. Melissa and Todd stood in the driveway, beside a faded olive green car that must have belonged to Todd.

Across the street, a blue hatchback pulled into Amy's driveway. Josh stepped out and started toward them.

"My riding lesson!" Callie said. "I completely forgot!" Just like she'd forgotten her history homework. She was so busy worrying about Star that she couldn't seem to remember anything else, even things she enjoyed, like her lessons. She jumped to her feet and ran to the door. Amy followed.

They met up with Josh right outside. His blond hair hung to his shoulders; as always, a battered cowboy hat covered his head.

"Forget something?" he asked Callie. He looked as much amused as annoyed. He was a lot like Amy that way.

"Sorry," Callie said. "I . . ." What excuse would make any sense? If her mom and dad

71

were there, they'd lecture Callie about taking her responsibilities more seriously.

But Josh wasn't like Callie's parents, not by a long shot. Sometimes Callie envied how laidback Amy's brother was. "Don't worry about it," Josh said. He took off his hat and ran a hand through his hair, looking suddenly tired. "The vet showed up halfway through what would have been your lesson, anyway."

Callie had forgotten that the vet was supposed to see Rusty today, too. "How is he?" she asked.

"Much better," Josh said. "The vet agrees the swelling is finally going down." He sighed. "I'd feel much better if I knew what spooked him to begin with, though. I've been riding that horse for years; I know he wasn't just frightened of some snake that got in his way." Josh put his hat back on and stared at Callie, his expression intense. "*You* don't remember anything unusual, do you? Anything at all that might have freaked the horses out?"

"No." Callie shifted uneasily. Lying to Josh was harder than lying to her parents, maybe because Josh didn't get angry if he didn't like what you said. He just really wanted to know what was going on. She suddenly felt guilty asking Amy to keep Star hidden from him. Yet what else could she do? She glanced at Amy for reassurance, but Amy just stared uncomfortably down at the ground.

Melissa looked up, saw Josh standing there, and called, "Hey, Josh, there's someone I want you to meet." She pulled Todd over. Callie was relieved; she didn't want to answer any more questions about their ride.

Josh listened politely as Todd was introduced. Todd, on the other hand, seemed a little tired of being shown around; he moved restlessly from one foot to the other as Melissa talked. Melissa seemed to have completely forgotten that just a few weeks before, she'd had a crush on Josh.

Callie's mother's car pulled into the driveway, and Melissa dragged Todd off to introduce him to her, too.

Josh shoved his hands into his pockets and looked at Amy. "I don't feel much like cooking tonight. How about you?"

Amy laughed. "Do I ever feel like cooking?"

"Right," Josh said with a smile. "Pizza it is." He looked at Callie. "Care to join us?"

"Sure," Callie said, then realized that if she went over there for dinner, it'd be hours before she got back to Star. Another car rumbled up along the dirt road. Dad pulled into the driveway behind Mom. With both her parents home, and Todd still around, Callie couldn't go out to Star now, anyway.

Callie sighed. As always, she'd have to wait until late at night, when everyone was asleep.

After dinner, Callie hung around with Amy and Josh for a while, talking and doing her homework.

Josh asked about their trail ride a few more times. Amy kept glancing at Callie, looking more and more unhappy as the evening went on, and Callie knew Amy still wished she could tell her brother the truth.

By the time Callie left, the sun had set. Amy walked her back home, reminding Callie that she'd agreed to take a turn watching Star. They decided that Amy would come by early in the morning, around two o'clock or so.

Amy took a deep breath. "With any luck, Josh'll be asleep the whole time that I'm gone."

Callie felt guilty again. If she just stayed out with Star herself, as least Amy wouldn't have to lie to her brother about anything else. "If you don't want to come—" she began.

"No," Amy said firmly. "I want to help. For Star's sake. And also for—" Amy cut the thought abruptly off, and said instead, "See you tonight?"

"Yeah." Callie yawned as she said good-bye to her friend. Much as she hated to leave Star partway through the night, much as she hated to make Amy sneak out, in a way she was glad

Amy had insisted on helping. Callie was already tired, and the thought of falling asleep outside again terrified her. She couldn't forget what had happened that morning, and what had happened in the afternoon, too.

Todd, as it turned out, had had dinner at Callie's house; he'd left not long before Callie returned home. When Callie walked in, Melissa was still talking about him, as she did her homework. He seemed nice enough, but how many times could someone repeat the same details about his green eyes, or his interest in soccer, or where he sat in math class, or anything else? Callie was already bored with him, and she'd only just met him.

Melissa spent so much time talking about Todd that she, Mom, and Dad stayed up much later than usual. Finally, though, everyone went to their rooms. As Callie crawled under the covers, she felt Star's presence, urging her to come out. Callie waited. Star's presence grew quieter, little more than a gentle whisper in Callie's mind, and she assumed the horse had accepted the fact that Callie couldn't go to her yet.

Finally, when she was sure her family was sleeping, Callie got up, quietly crossed the living room and the kitchen, and walked out the patio door. She didn't risk climbing out the window again, not after her father had caught her the last time. She rounded the corner of the house, looked around the yard for Star—and nearly screamed at what she saw.

Over by the corral, Star lay on the ground, barely moving.

Callie's breath caught in her throat. She bolted across the yard, fearing that, ghost or not, Star somehow had died, that her illness her killed her. Horses weren't supposed to just lie down, were they?

As Callie neared Star, the horse snorted, stretched her legs out beneath her, and slowly stood. She staggered, then got her footing more steadily, and walked up to Callie. The mare looked straight at her, not seeming concerned, just tired. Callie felt that weariness; it made her more tired, too. What would have happened if she hadn't come out right then? Would Star ever have gotten up? Callie shuddered. She couldn't get the image of Star, lying so still, out of her head. She wrapped her arm around Star's neck and held on tightly. For a long time they just stood together like that.

Star nudged her head up against Callie. Callie saw a brief image of the two of them running through the wash, and she knew Star wanted more badly than ever to ride.

Yet Callie still felt the horse's exhaustion. She ran a hand through Star's mane, felt the gritty dust embedded there. Star wasn't back to normal, not by a long shot, even ignoring the awful way she'd been lying on the ground. Riding would only make things worse.

Instead, Callie took Star's reins and led her down to the wash. Star sighed, accepting that, even though Callie knew she'd still rather ride. Together they walked along the sandy ground. The night was silent and dark, peaceful. The wind had died down to little more than a breeze. Even as ill as Star was, her slow, silky gait was calming somehow. The horse kept stopping to lean her head on Callie's shoulder or simply to stare out at her, and that was soothing, too. By the time Callie returned to her yard, she felt better.

She found Amy waiting for them and told her what had happened. To Callie's surprise, Amy didn't seem all that concerned. She pushed her hands down into her pockets. "Star was probably just sleeping," Amy said. She kept her voice low, so that no one in the house would hear. "Horses sleep lying down sometimes, though people who haven't seen them do that before worry when they see it. It'd only be a problem if she didn't get up on her own after a while."

Callie didn't admit she'd been worried about just that. She still couldn't dismiss Star's lying down as easily as Amy had. Finally she realized why. "Star doesn't sleep," Callie said. At least, she never had before.

"Oh," Amy said. "I'd forgotten about that." For a while they stood in silence, Callie with her arm draped over Star's neck, Amy staring at the horse. Was sleeping part of Star's becoming more like a normal, nonghostly horse? Or was it another stage of her illness, with Star becoming so tired she couldn't even stay awake all the time? If Star could sleep, could she somehow lose consciousness for longer than that? Again Callie wondered how much longer she had before Star's thoughts were somehow lost to her forever. She drew her arms around herself, more worried than ever.

Amy dug one foot into the ground. "You should get some sleep," she said.

If Callie went to sleep, would Star still be there when she woke up? She told herself that of course she would be, but she felt funnier than ever about leaving her.

"Don't worry, I'll take good care of her," Amy said. "And I'll try to see if I can figure out anything else about what's wrong."

Callie shifted awkwardly and looked at Star. "Will you be all right with Amy?" she asked. Star only moved closer to Callie in response. Callie hugged her, stifling a yawn as she did. Amy was right; Callie needed to sleep sometime. She took a deep breath, then turned and started to walk away, toward the patio door. After only a few steps she looked back. Star snorted and pawed the ground. Amy reached for Star's reins, but Star turned her head away.

It's all right, Callie thought. She pictured Amy staying out there with Star, while she went inside. Callie tried to reassure Star that this was okay. Star looked back and forth between Callie and Amy, her ears twitching every which way. Then Callie pictured herself sitting by her bedroom window, not very far from Star at all. Star hesitated, then accepted that. She turned gently back toward Amy and rested her head on her shoulder. Even in the dark, Callie saw the grin that lit up Amy's face. She smiled and went inside.

She changed into a nightgown and knelt right by her window, just as she'd promised Star. For a while she stayed awake, watching Star and Amy standing together. Amy began working her fingers through Star's mane, puling out tangles, her gaze never leaving the horse. Star just stood there, very still and patient, her own eyes on the window through which she could see Callie.

Star and Amy would be fine together. Callie thought about crawling into bed, but knowing Star was watching her, she couldn't bring herself to move any farther away. Still kneeling by the window, Callie drifted off to the comfortable feeling of Star's presence and the sound of Amy whispering to the horse.

She woke to a muffled yell from Amy—and the feeling from Star that something was terribly wrong.

Chapter Seven

Callie leaped to her feet, opened the window, and pulled out the screen. A gust of warm air blew in, tugging at her nightgown. Callie jumped out the window and looked wildly around.

Out near the wash, Amy lay huddled on the ground. For a second Callie couldn't see Star at all. Then Star turned visible again, but very faint, a translucent shimmer in the dark night. She was upset and scared; Callie felt it. Star almost seemed as if she were trying to stay solid, but failing.

Callie ran across the yard. Rocks cut her bare feet, and wind blew her nightgown around, but she didn't care. Behind her, she heard the cottonwood and mesquite trees blowing about. Dust flew up into Callie's face, but she ignored it. As she ran, Star's frantic thoughts flickered in and out of her mind, making her fear she didn't have much time before Star disappeared for good.

She ran down into the wash and threw herself at Star. At first her arms passed through empty air, but then she felt the horse, solid and silky, beneath her. She felt something else, too, a strange tug, as if something were trying to pull her and Star away—to where she wasn't sure.

Callie dug her toes firmly into the sand, resisting the pull. Star sighed, an incredibly weary sound, as though resisting were the last thing she wanted to do. Gray mist began to swirl around them. When Callie looked down at herself, she wasn't surprised, only quietly horrified, to see that she was shimmering as strongly as Star was. The tugging grew stronger. She felt a clammy chill between her shoulders, as if someone were running cold, wet fingers down her back.

Beyond the gray, behind her, Callie heard something: Amy, sobbing softly. In her rush to keep Star from disappearing, she'd completely forgotten about her friend. She hadn't even stopped to see if Amy was okay. How could Callie have run right past her like that?

Especially since, as far as Callie could remember, she'd never heard Amy cry before. Not when she was frightened, not when she was hurt, not ever. Amy was the one who said you had to laugh to cope with serious things.

Callie let go of Star and turned around, looking for her friend. Outside the wash, just a short distance away, Amy still lay curled up on the ground. As Callie stared at her the chilly touch between her shoulders disappeared; the tugging stopped; the gray rolled away like sea foam, toward the edge of her vision. It didn't disappear completely this time, though. At the very edges of Callie's sight, so faint that she couldn't focus on them directly, a few tendrils remained. She ignored them for now and ran out of the wash to kneel by Amy's side. Faint dawn light touched the sky, making the night not quite as black as before.

"Are you okay?" Callie asked. "What's wrong?"

Amy looked up, saw Callie, and cried harder. Her clothes were covered with dust, her face splotched with tears. She looked like maybe she'd fallen. Callie stared at her friend, wondering again how she could have possibly ignored her.

"It didn't work," Amy whispered, so low that Callie strained to hear.

"What didn't work?" Callie asked.

Amy looked back down to the ground. "If I tell you, you have to promise not to get angry."

Star walked up behind Callie. Callie heard the horse's tired, heavy panting, combined with a new irregular wheezing sound. Star stretched her head down toward Callie, and Callie felt the horse's warm breath on the back of her neck. What would have happened if Callie hadn't shown up when she did? She drew her arms tightly around herself at the thought, but didn't turn away from Amy.

"What would I get angry about?" she asked her friend.

Amy brushed a hand across her forehead, leaving a smudge of dirt behind. "I tried to ride Star," she whispered.

"What?" Callie's voice came out as a strangled yell; she struggled to lower it. "You did what?" Amy knew Star was too sick to ride. How could she do something that might make Star worse? It was true that Amy had always wanted to ride Star, but with all she knew about horses, didn't she know better than to try now? Besides, it was bad enough that Callie hadn't been able to ride for the past few days; it wasn't fair that someone else, even Amy, should ride instead.

"I'm sorry," Amy said. "I hope I didn't hurt her. I didn't mean to. I—" She choked on a hiccup, and her voice trailed off.

Callie wanted to jump up and scream at Amy, but that would wake her family. She wanted to demand that Amy explain why she'd even think about trying such a crazy thing. Yet she still felt awful for her friend, huddled up like that, looking so miserable. "Why'd you do it?" Callie asked, as calmly and quietly as she could.

Amy took a deep breath. "Because of my parents."

"What?" Callie just looked at her. "What do you mean?"

Amy sighed. The knees of her jeans were torn, and her hands were scraped, too. "It sounds so stupid when I try to explain. But, well, you know I've always kind of wondered—" Her voice cracked. She paused, then started again. "Star's a ghost, right?"

"Yeah," Callie said, wondering what that had to do with anything.

"Well, I've always hoped Mom and Dad might still be ghosts somewhere, too. I thought maybe Star could lead me to them." Amy's eyes turned suddenly intense. "I did see my parents, you know, just for a few seconds, not long after they died. In my room, right outside the doorway. But they left before I could say anything. If I could talk to them, Callie, even only for a minute or two—" Amy swallowed, leaving her sentence unfinished.

As always, hearing Amy talk about her parents twisted Callie's stomach into a tight knot. She couldn't picture her own parents suddenly not being there. "So you tried to ride Star to find them?" Callie asked.

Amy nodded. "I thought maybe I could find them in that gray place you talked about. I had to try."

Wisps of gray still hovered at the edges of Callie's sight. She remembered the tug she'd felt, trying to pull her somewhere. She didn't want to know where. "You don't want to go there," Callie said.

Amy looked up at her. "Yes, I do," she said, her voice very serious. "If there's any chance at all that Mom and Dad might be there." She went on, "But I tried. And it didn't work. Star got uneasy as soon as I put my foot in the stirrup. I managed to swing up onto her back, even walk for a few steps; but then she disappeared out from under me. One moment I was riding, the next I was falling through empty air, and Star was shimmering and fading and running away." Amy drew her knees up to her chin. Callie stared at her friend in uncomfortable silence.

Finally Callie stood. Star, still right behind her, leaned her head heavily on Callie's shoulder. Callie felt the horse's confusion at all that had happened, and also her deep weariness. She was still wheezing, too. She really was worse off now that Amy had tried to ride her. Callie looked from Amy to Star and back to Amy again. She wasn't sure how to feel. She felt bad for both Amy and Star at the same time.

Eventually Amy stood, as well. The faint beginnings of dawn had given way to a pale pink that touched everything around them. Amy stared out at the mountains, as if searching for something. "I know they're out there, somewhere," she whispered. "I don't know why I can't ever see them, but—well, sometimes I can almost feel them watching me, you know?"

Callie shivered. Could her friend really sense her parents, the same way Callie sensed Star? Or did Amy just want to badly enough that she thought she did?

Somewhere beyond the house, Callie heard someone calling. She tensed, fearing that her dad or mom had discovered her open window again, even though they usually weren't up quite so early.

"It's Josh," Amy said. "He's always up early for work." She swallowed. "I need to go. I don't know what I'll tell him. I don't know—" She took a deep breath, and her whole body shook. "I just hate all this sometimes, you know?" She turned abruptly away and ran across Callie's yard.

Callie clenched her hands by her sides, trying to keep from trembling herself. She wanted to run after Amy, but her feet felt frozen to the ground. She couldn't do anything but stare after her friend. What could she possibly say or do to make everything all right? A voice in the back of her head said she should at least try something, anything, but then Amy disappeared around the side of the house.

Callie sighed and turned to Star. "Could you really have taken Amy to her parents?" she asked. "If you were healthy and all?" Star stared back at her through tired, watery eyes, unable to answer.

Callie heard Josh and Amy out front, talking in low tones as they walked back across the street. Her own parents would be awake soon, too. She hugged Star tightly. So far they'd been lucky; whenever something had been wrong with Star, Callie had been around to help her. But what would happen if she was somewhere else the next time something happened, maybe at school or a riding lesson? What would she do then?

"I don't want to leave you," Callie said. Star snorted, as if agreeing. Callie felt the horse's tired thoughts pulling at her, begging her to stay.

"I'll be back," Callie promised. *Stay hidden*, she thought. She walked slowly back toward the house. Star didn't follow. When Callie looked back, she was walking along the edge of the wash instead, away from the house. The edge of the sun poked up over the mountains, casting gold light over the entire yard, making Star's gray coat almost seem to shine again. Then Star stumbled over a tree root, and the moment was broken, the mare's coat dusty and dull once more.

Callie watched Star—who she'd never seen stumble at all before—regain her footing and continue walking away. A wave of loneliness swept from Star over Callie. The feeling stayed with Callie as she walked the rest of the way to the house.

So did the tendrils of gray mist. When Callie tried to look at them directly, they almost disappeared, but when she ignored them, they drew closer to her.

Callie blinked fiercely, over and over again, but the mist wouldn't go away.

Chapter Eight

An hour later, as Callie showered and dressed, the gray was still with her. She tried to ignore it, but when she did the tendrils only grew thicker and darker, reaching toward her with long, ghostly fingers. When she turned to face the tendrils head-on, they backed off a little, but as soon as she turned her attention to other things, they stretched toward her once again. She wished they would just go away.

Star's loneliness stayed with Callie, too. She kept seeing flashes of what Star was doing— walking carefully around some cholla and prickly pear, sniffing at bushes, skittering backward as a quail crossed her path. Callie wondered whether Star saw her, as well.

She went into the kitchen to get breakfast. Mom stood by the kitchen counter, pouring herself some coffee. At the table, Melissa sat across from Dad, talking. The gray tendrils distracted Callie, making it hard to focus on any of them very clearly. For a moment she couldn't quite make out Melissa's words. She forced herself to listen harder, and the gray backed off a bit. Callie felt a cold touch on her shoulder; then that, too, backed away.

"Todd called a little while ago," Melissa told her father between bites of toast. "He wants to give me a ride to school today, if that's okay with you guys."

"Well, if you're sure he's a safe driver—" Dad began.

"Of course he is," Melissa said. She spoke politely enough, but Callie saw a flash of anger in her eyes. Melissa hated it when anyone said anything bad about boys she liked. "He's had his license for months now."

Callie poured herself a bowl of cereal and sat down. Mom walked over with her coffee a moment later. "Maybe Todd can drop Callie off, too," she suggested.

Melissa's face sank at the idea. "That's okay," Callie said quickly. She didn't exactly want to be stuck in a car with Melissa and Todd, anyway. "I'd really rather just take the bus."

The doorbell rang. "That's him!" Melissa jumped up and dumped her plate in the sink. "Thanks," she whispered to Callie as she ran back past the table to answer the door. Callie heard Todd's voice from the doorway. "See you guys later!" Melissa called, then disappeared outside. What would she have done if their parents hadn't given her permission to ride with Todd?

Within a few minutes, Mom and Dad were on their way to work. Callie was the last one out the door. She locked it behind her.

Amy arrived at the bus stop several minutes after Callie. She wore clean jeans now, and the dirt from her fall had been washed away, but still, she looked exhausted.

Callie was awake for once. Then again, with creepy gray fingers lurking at the edge of her sight, the thought of dozing off, even for a few seconds, terrified her.

Amy looked at the ground, avoiding Callie's gaze. Callie shifted from one foot to the other, still not quite sure what to say. Finally she asked, "Was Josh really mad at you for being out so early?"

Amy seemed a little startled at that. "No," she said. "Just curious what I was up to."

Callie tensed. "You didn't tell him about—"

"Of course not!" Amy whirled to face her, her brown eyes angry. "I told you I wouldn't say anything, didn't I? When I say things I mean them, Callie." Her voice dropped. "Besides, you know I wouldn't do anything to hurt Star."

Yet Amy had ridden Star, even knowing how sick she was. Callie stared at her friend, and Amy glanced away from her. Awkward silence stretched between them. To break it up, Callie finally asked, "What *did* you tell Josh?"

Amy bit her lip. "I told him you and I went out for an early walk. I told him I tripped while we were walking, and that's why my jeans were torn."

"Did he believe you?"

Amy shook her head. "A story like that? Of course not. But he didn't call me on it, either. He just listened while I explained. Then he reminded me he was always around if I needed to talk, and he dropped it." Amy ran a hand through her hair. "I almost wish he would have gotten angry instead, you know?"

"I guess." Callie more often wished her parents wouldn't get angry.

"Josh tries so hard to understand things, to make up for Mom and Dad . . ." Amy's voice trailed off. The bus turned the corner and headed toward them. They got on without another word, Callie taking the first empty window seat she could find, and Amy sitting beside her.

Ricky was across the aisle again. "Hey," he said, leaning toward them, "I couldn't find that horse yesterday." His voice held an accusing edge. "I checked all around your neighborhood, but none of the horses I saw looked anything like that one. Where'd you say the new people who owned her lived?"

A strange look crossed Amy's face. "I don't know," she said in a small, strangled voice. "I don't know." She buried her head in her hands and began to cry again, soft, choking sobs.

Callie's throat tightened; she felt about to cry herself. "I'm sorry," she whispered, not sure whether she was sorry about Amy's trying to ride, or about her parents, or even about her having to lie again to Ricky right then. Amy didn't answer, didn't look up at all.

Ricky glanced across the seat to Callie, a questioning look on his face. Callie just shrugged. Ricky scowled at her, and Callie got the feeling that even though he didn't know what was wrong, he blamed her for it. She glared at him, then turned away to look out the window.

She saw bright blue sky, gray tendrils still swirling at its edges. She wondered if Star saw the tendrils, too. Did the horse know anything more than Callie about where they had come from?

As if in response, Callie saw a flash of Star walking along a wash somewhere, a wider, deeper wash than the one in her yard. A jogger ran along the sand in Star's general direction. Star stepped silently up onto the bank, hiding among a cluster of palo verdes that bordered a housing development. She seemed to blend in with the trees, a silent gray shadow against a background of green. The jogger didn't even glance her way as he panted past.

When he was out of sight, Star returned to the wash and kept walking, head low, leaving hoofprints in the sand behind her. A breeze blew her mane about her neck, but she barely noticed. Her deep eyes were intent on the path in front of her. A lizard scuttled by, but her ears didn't perk up; she just kept walking. Callie had no idea where Star was going, but she seemed to have some deliberate destination in mind.

At one point Star slowed way down, breathing hard, and didn't return to normal walking speed for several minutes. Another time she began to shimmer silver-gray, so that Callie saw the wash right through her. The image of Star began to flicker in and out. Callie gripped the edge of the window so tightly the metal hurt her palms, not letting go until Star came into focus once more.

When the bus pulled into school, Callie almost couldn't make herself follow everyone else toward the building; she wanted to go off and look for Star instead. As she started walking, she saw Ricky tap Amy on the shoulder and start quietly talking to her. Suddenly, she felt as if she really were just some newcomer, who didn't belong in Tucson or anywhere else.

She turned fiercely away from them both and hurried inside.

All through that morning the gray tendrils lurked at the edges of Callie's sight, reaching toward her whenever she stopped paying attention to them. They kept distracting her, so that she had trouble focusing on anything else. In homeroom, when Ms. Trujillo called her name, she didn't notice at first. In history class Mr. Johnson had to repeat a question three times before Callie heard him—and when she did, she didn't know the answer. And in the halls, as the other kids jostled her about, Callie kept feeling clammy fingers brushing against her neck, her arms, her legs.

At lunch, too, Callie couldn't focus. Amy still looked tired, but she laughed as she poked at her food and talked with Alicia and Matt about some football game at the high school. She didn't ignore Callie, but she didn't go out of her way to talk to her, either. Ricky paid no attention at all to Callie for once, muttering as he read a chapter of his science book.

Callie looked out the windows, at the bright blue sky. She saw Star again, stumbling across dark asphalt somewhere. She heard Alicia's voice, saying, "Are you feeling okay, Callie? You look kind of pale."

"I'm fine." Callie brushed a hand across her forehead; it felt clammy and cold, too. As her hand came away, she saw that the skin was shimmering. Across the table, Amy's mouth fell open; she quickly closed it again. Panic caught at the back of Callie's throat. What would happen if she faded out right here, in school? "I just need a drink of water," she said, grasping for some excuse to get away from everyone. She stood and started across the cafeteria, toward the water fountain. Her legs shook, and she stopped to steady them. She glanced out the windows again, and for a moment she thought she saw Star in the schoolyard, staring at her with large, dark eyes.

"Hey!" someone shouted. "Look at that horse!"

Star *was* in the schoolyard. Callie wasn't just seeing a vision of her this time.

A door stood to one side of the windows. Callie ran toward it. Other people started in the same direction; the door was already open by the time she got there. Outside, a bunch of kids stood uneasily in a semicircle, watching Star. Star was shimmering slightly, just like Callie; maybe that was why no one had walked up to her yet. Through her, Callie faintly saw the black asphalt of the schoolyard.

Star lifted her head as Callie ran toward her. Her ears perked up; her tired eyes seemed to brighten, just a little. Callie kept running, pushing past the other kids to grab Star tightly.

Callie felt Star's joy at seeing her. The horse had followed her, all the way to school, just to be with her. Star nudged at Callie's shoulder; Callie hugged her even tighter, inhaling her sweet cut-grass smell, not wanting to ever let go.

"Do you know that horse?" some girl asked.

Callie abruptly released her hold on Star, feeling Star's confusion as she did. "Um, no. Of course not." As soon as she spoke, she realized how ridiculous that sounded. More kids stood in the schoolyard now, staring at her. Callie looked around at them, feeling trapped.

Star picked up on the trapped feeling. Callie felt panic rise in the mare's mind. Star's ears went flat against her head. She nickered and whirled around, bolting through the crowd. Her mane flew wildly out behind her. Her ears darted frantically about as she ran. A couple of kids jumped out of her way. Star ran across the schoolyard, through the open chain-link fence, and out into the street.

For a few seconds more she shimmered bright gray, like storm clouds with sun behind them. Then she turned solid as any frightened horse. Her hooves clattered against the asphalt. The sound faded as she disappeared around a corner. Callie almost ran after her, but she knew she couldn't catch up with any running horse, let alone Star. She looked down at her hands, saw that they, too, were solid once more.

The kids all started talking at once. A teacher stepped out into the schoolyard and asked what was going on. In the confusion that followed, Callie slipped back into the cafeteria. Several kids turned to watch her go. She doubted anyone believed she knew nothing about Star now. She just hoped no one would tell the teacher.

Once Callie was inside, Amy stepped up behind her, asking, "Are you okay?" Callie just nodded. "How about Star?" Amy asked.

In her mind, Callie saw Star running through an empty, dusty lot, stumbling more and more often as she ran. Suddenly her legs gave way beneath her, and she tumbled to the ground. Callie gasped out loud. For a moment Star just lay on her side, as still and unmoving as she'd been when she'd slept last night, and Callie feared this time she might really never get up. Then, much too slowly, Star staggered to her feet. Her legs and right side were all scraped up. She barely looked able to walk, but after a few steps she broke into a rough, uneven gait, somewhere between a trot and a canter. Callie swallowed hard, leaving Amy's question unanswered.

"If there's anything I can to do help . . ." Amy's voice trailed off. Callie and Amy stared awkwardly at each other. Did Callie still trust

Amy with Star after what had happened? She wasn't sure.

Other kids made their way back into the cafeteria. Afraid someone would point her out to the teacher, Callie crossed the cafeteria toward the other door, the one that led to the hallway. Amy followed. The bell rang.

"See you after school?" Amy asked.

"I guess," Callie said. She watched Amy walk out into the hall, then started toward her own locker. She opened it and stared wearily at the books inside.

Someone reached out and slammed her locker door shut in front of her, with a clang of rattling metal. Callie looked up and saw Ricky standing there, arms across his chest.

"What's going on?" he demanded.

Callie shook her head. Ricky was the last person she wanted to deal with right now. "What do you mean?" she asked.

Ricky gave her a long, suspicious look. "That horse outside the cafeteria was the exact same one I saw by your house the day before yesterday. The one you said lived near you, but that I couldn't find anywhere. You don't really expect me to believe you when you say you've never seen her before, do you?"

Callie wished he'd just leave her alone already. "I don't care what you think," she said.

Ricky smirked. "You could have fooled me."

His eyes narrowed. "Something strange is going on. If you won't tell me what, I'll find out on my own." He turned and disappeared down the hall without another word.

Callie sighed. She was worried about what Ricky might find out, but she was more worried about Star. She saw the horse again, not running now, but walking slowly, staggering every few steps, strongly favoring her left legs. She was tired and she was hurt. Callie couldn't just leave her alone out there, not now.

Go home, Callie thought. She pictured her backyard. Star turned in a direction Callie hoped was toward the house. Sweat rolled down her coat; her sides heaved raggedly in and out.

Leaving her locker door closed, Callie turned and walked away. Other kids bumped into her as she passed them, but she didn't care.

The bell rang again, but Callie didn't go to class. Instead, she stepped outside, and like Star, started for home.

Chapter Nine

Callie felt guilty as she crept away from the school and even guiltier when no one saw her leave or tried to stop her. She'd never left school without permission before. She didn't see any choice, but it still felt wrong. She almost turned around and went back in, but she thought about Star, pushed her guilt aside, and kept walking.

The bus ride between home and school took only about fifteen minutes. Callie knew walking would take longer, but she hadn't realized how much longer. As she walked, the sun burned her bare arms and legs; heat parched her throat. A hot, steady wind picked up, drying out her skin and cracking her lips. And gray tendrils still swirled at the edges of her sight, making her feel even more guilty and edgy somehow.

Star got home a lot faster than Callie did, in spite of the fact that she was hurt. After about half an hour, Callie saw a vision of Star in the yard, out by her old corral, waiting. Almost an hour after that, Callie came to her own front door. She hadn't expected it to take anywhere near that long to get back. By then her throat ached every time she swallowed. She felt dizzy, too, as though she might collapse if she stayed out in the sun much longer.

She wanted to run right out to Star, but first she desperately needed water. She unlocked the door—the relatively cool indoor air felt wonderful against her dry skin—and stumbled into the kitchen. *I'm here,* she thought to Star, as she filled her glass of water. Callie felt how exhausted Star was, but she felt the horse's joy at her presence, too.

Callie drank two glasses before her throat felt better and the dizziness subsided. She stood for a moment more inside, then walked out the patio door.

As she stepped around the side of the house, Star staggered up to meet her. The horse's side and legs were still scratched up, scraped raw in some places, much worse than the times Callie had skinned her own knees and elbows. Dirt was embedded deep in the scratches. Callie winced, feeling deep within herself how badly Star hurt. "I'm sorry," Callie whispered, though as with Amy, she felt helpless to do anything but stand there with Star.

Star leaned against Callie, more heavily than usual, as if wanting physical support as much as the comfort of Callie's presence. Callie draped her arms over Star's back. Her feet ached from walking, and the sun had turned her arms so red they ached. She lost track of how long she and Star stood together like that. Hot wind blew through the cottonwoods, making a sound like falling rain, even though the monsoons that had drenched the desert less than a week ago seemed ages away now.

Eventually Callie stepped back, knowing she had to at least try to treat Star's injuries. She touched one of the raw, dirt-encrusted scrapes, felt Star cringe as she did. Callie wasn't sure whether Star's scrapes could get infected, but at least cleaning them out was something she knew how to deal with, unlike all the different symptoms of Star's illness. She released her hold on Star and ran into the house, grabbing her family's first-aid kit from the bathroom. As she stepped back into the yard, she heard the bus rumble to a stop in front of the house.

"Callie!" Amy ran around the corner to her, breathing hard. "You're all right!"

"Yeah," Callie said, wondering why Amy would expect her not to be. She was hot and sore and tired, but that would all go away eventually. She was much more worried about Star right now.

Amy swallowed. "When you didn't show up on the bus, I thought you'd gone."

"I had gone," Callie admitted. "I'd gone home."

"That's not what I meant." Amy shook her head. "I thought you'd faded out. Gone away with Star, for good this time." An angry edge crept into Amy's voice. "You scared me. I don't want you to disappear and never come back."

Callie turned to face her friend, still clutching the first-aid kit in one hand. "Well, I wouldn't have wanted you to leave last night, either." She suddenly knew that this was another reason—maybe even the biggest one—she'd been so upset when Amy had tried to ride. What if she'd succeeded? What if somehow she'd gone away for good? Callie didn't want to lose Star, but just as badly, she didn't want to lose Amy.

Amy looked down at her feet, kicked up a small cloud of dust. "If I'd left that would have been different."

"Would it?" Callie asked. Amy didn't answer. Callie swallowed, her throat tightening as she did. "Well, I'm glad you're here now," she said, her voice strange and hoarse.

Amy smiled faintly. "Yeah. Me too." Without warning, she reached out and hugged her friend. Callie dropped the first-aid kit and hugged Amy back, as tightly as she could. Her eyes stung, and she knew she was crying, but she didn't care. Star walked up to them, gently nudging Callie's shoulder. Callie smiled at the touch of the horse's warm, damp nose.

Callie heard a sudden movement. A few feet away from her, someone cleared his throat. Callie wiped her eyes on the back of her hand, stepped away from Amy, and looked up.

Ricky stood in the yard, staring straight at Star. "It's that horse again," he said. "I knew it." Callie wondered how long he'd been watching her. He had no right to be there, but he didn't seem to care. He shoved his hands deep into his pockets. "What's going on?" he demanded.

Callie's stomach clenched into a knot. "Nothing," she said.

"Yeah, right." Ricky laughed out loud this time. Amy glanced nervously back and forth between her friends, as if trapped between them.

Callie tried to think of some explanation, but for once she couldn't come up with anything. She only knew that she didn't want Ricky anywhere near Star, didn't want him to even know about the horse. At least when Melissa had found out about Star, it had been for a reason, because Melissa needed to ride to shelter. Ricky was snooping around for no reason at all. "It's none of your business," Callie said.

"Where'd she come from? And what are you

doing, just keeping her in your backyard, without a corral or fences or anything?" Ricky's face turned serious, and angry as well. "Maybe back in New York, where you never see real animals, you think you can do that. Out here people know better."

Callie glared at him. "What makes you think there aren't real animals in New York? And what makes you think I don't know about horses?" For someone who kept complaining about out-of-towners, he didn't seem to know a whole lot about them.

"Well, you sure aren't taking very good care of this horse." Ricky walked up to Star, gesturing toward her scrapes and bruises. Star sneezed at him, getting horse snot all over his jacket.

"I am too taking care of her!" Callie said. Then she clamped her mouth shut. She'd just admitted that she knew about Star after all.

"Callie knows what she's doing," Amy said suddenly. Ricky turned to look at her, as if realizing for the first time that she might know as much as Callie did.

"What's going on?" Ricky demanded again. Neither Callie nor Amy answered. Star turned away and sniffed at a pile of dirt, as if a bit bored with their whole conversation. She began to walk across the yard, still stumbling as she did.

Ricky shook his head. "I'm calling animal

control. Someone has to let them know about this. You might not care one way or the other, Callie from New York, but some of us don't like seeing animals abused, especially by stupid out-of-towners." He started toward Star, as if ready to turn her in himself. He approached her very slowly, from behind.

Star's ears went flat against her head. Callie knew from experience that meant she was about to kick. She leaped after Ricky and pushed him out of the way. They fell to the ground, just as Star's rear legs kicked out through the space where they'd been. Star nickered and ran.

Ricky shoved Callie off him and stood. "What'd you do that for?"

Callie stood, as well. "You say *I* don't know about animals? Don't you even know that horses spook when you sneak up on them?"

Star nickered again. Callie felt her uneasiness. The horse skittered to a stop at the edge of the wash and whirled around, eyeing everyone nervously.

Callie had come home in the first place to take care of Star, and here she was wasting time arguing with Ricky. She turned away from him, picked up the first-aid kit, and ran across the yard to the horse. Amy and Ricky both followed, but Callie barely noticed.

As she ran the gray tendrils thickened again,

clouding her sight, becoming a misty veil between her and the rest of the world. As she approached Star, the veil parted to let her reach the horse, then enveloped them both. Callie saw Star shimmering brightly. The mare's legs shook, as if she were about to collapse again. Callie held Star tightly, willing the horse to keep standing. She didn't need to look to know that she was shimmering as brightly as Star. She felt a cold touch, not just chilly fingers but also the palm of a hand, gripping the back of her neck. The cold spread down beneath her T-shirt.

A low moaning sound started up, almost human but not quite, from all directions at once. The sound scraped against Callie's bones, like fingernails against a blackboard. Were there words in that sound? She strained to hear, but the sound faded to little more than a whisper as she did.

"Callie!" Amy called. At the sound of her voice the moaning faded, the veil thinned, and the cold hand let go. Callie's arms ached with sunburn once more. When she reached out to stroke Star's shoulder, the mare seemed perfectly solid.

Amy looked nervous, though, as if she wasn't sure Callie and Star would remain solid for long. Callie wanted to reassure her, but she didn't know how long she'd remain solid, either.

The anger drained slowly out of Ricky's face. He even looked a little bit frightened now. He must have seen Callie begin to fade, too. He pulled his jacket tightly around him. "What," he demanded slowly, "just happened?"

"What do you mean?" Callie asked, hoping somehow to get out of answering.

"One minute you and that horse were there, and the next you almost weren't." Ricky stared at her, and Callie knew that he wasn't going to just go away, and he wasn't going to believe any excuse she gave him. He knew what he'd seen, after all.

Maybe he wouldn't believe the truth, either. Maybe he'd decide she was crazy and finally leave her and Star alone. Callie took a deep breath. "Star's a ghost," she said.

Amy's mouth fell open. She stared at Callie, eyes wide, as if she couldn't believe that Callie had really just blurted Star's secret, after she'd worked so hard to keep it hidden. There was no way for Callie to explain why she'd done that, not here, so she just stood there, waiting for Ricky to laugh again.

Instead, his face turned even paler, and his eyes grew wide. "She's a *what*?" He backed away, as if suddenly terrified of Star. He took a deep breath, closed his eyes, and opened them again. "What's she doing here? Can't you get rid of her?"

"Get rid of her?" Callie reached out and gripped Star's mane. "Why would I want to get rid of her?" Threatening to call animal control was bad enough. "You're the one who was just complaining that she wasn't being taken care of."

"That was before I knew what she was." Ricky took another step back.

"What's wrong with you?" Callie asked. How could anyone be so frightened of Star?

"Wrong with *me*?" Ricky said. "You're the one who's crazy. Don't you know how dangerous ghosts are?"

"Dangerous?" Callie's voice rose. "Star's not dangerous!" Callie tightened her hold on Star. Star leaned in closer, as if to emphasize Callie's point.

Ricky just shook his head. "Ghosts make all sorts of bad things happen. They scare you, they make you sick—" Ricky's eyes widened. "No wonder you always look so tired. It's because of her, isn't it?" He pointed at Star.

"I'm tired because I'm not getting enough sleep," Callie snapped. She wasn't getting enough sleep because of Star, but that was different. "What makes you think ghosts are dangerous, anyway?"

"They're dead," Ricky said. "They don't belong here. They get jealous of the living, all sorts of things. My family's told me a few stories, but mostly it's just common sense."

Callie remembered Michael, Star's original owner, getting jealous of the time Callie spent with Star. First he'd kept Star from seeing Callie; then he'd followed Star and Callie into the mountains, scaring Callie by sneaking around watching her from the woods. But he hadn't actually been dangerous, as far as Callie could tell.

Ricky glanced at Star, then quickly looked away. "The living and the dead just don't belong together. Isn't that obvious?"

"No," Callie said.

Amy bit her lip, as if considering something. "What sort of stories have your folks told you?" she asked.

"What does it matter?" Callie demanded. "None of this has anything to do with Star." She grabbed Star's reins. If Ricky wouldn't leave her alone, she'd just take Star and go somewhere else.

Amy put a hand on Callie's shoulder, stopping her. "Something's wrong with Star," she said softly. "Neither of us has been able to figure out what. Maybe Ricky knows something that would help."

Callie scowled. Amy kept staring at Ricky. "What do you know about ghosts?" Amy asked him.

Ricky looked down, avoiding her gaze. "Mostly just about people who've gotten ill when they've seen ghosts. This one family back on the rez—the reservation—moved out of their house after one of the kids saw a ghost there, because they were so worried about what could happen."

"Star doesn't go around making anyone sick," Callie snapped. "All she's done since I've moved here is help me. She's not some evil spirit, whatever you think. She's a good spirit. Haven't you ever heard of those?"

Ricky looked back up at her. "Sure I have. But good spirits are different from ghosts."

"Different how?" Callie demanded.

"Spirits don't come from people that were alive once," Ricky said. "They don't even look like us."

"Star doesn't look like us, either," Callie said. "She's a horse."

Ricky threw his arms up at that. "You know what I mean."

"So tell us about these good spirits," Amy said.

Ricky looked from Callie to Amy and back again. He seemed even more uncomfortable than before. "What do you expect?" he asked. "That I'm going do dig up some old Indian story that'll solve all your problems? It doesn't work that way, you know, whatever tourists and easterners think. It's not that simple." He gestured toward Amy. "You should know that, at least."

"I do know it's not that simple," Amy said. "But it couldn't hurt, could it?" When Ricky didn't answer, she went on, "You keep saying you think ghosts are dangerous, but you won't say anything about how or why. If you want us to be more careful, you have to tell us more." A wry smile crossed Amy's face. "Then at least anything we do will be our own fault."

Ricky hesitated, as if considering that. "Well, even good spirits can cause trouble, you know? But I don't know any of the stories as well as I should, not well enough to tell them properly to anyone else. If I'd grown up on the rez, it'd be different, but living here in Tucson . . ." Ricky shrugged. He was silent for a moment, and Callie thought he'd decided not to tell them anything after all. He glanced at Star, and Callie knew the horse's presence still made him nervous.

"The spirits are called the *Gahn*," he said abruptly. He pronounced the word oddly, with more of an accent than his other words; Callie wasn't sure she could have repeated it quite right. "They're mountain spirits, sent a long time ago to show the Apache how to live." Ricky kicked at the dirt with his sneaker. "That's one reason I'm not sure it makes any sense to tell you any of this. Part of the point is that they're Apache spirits. I don't know what sort of spirits would be sent to help anyone else."

He took a breath. "But anyway, the *Gahn* lived among the Apache for years and years. Eventually they got tired of being around people, though, and they returned to the mountains that they'd come from. So now it's sort of like they have their world and we have ours."

Callie tightened her grip on Star's reins. Star was nothing like the spirits Ricky was talking about. Star wanted to be with Callie.

"There's this one story about the *Gahn* I remember," Ricky said, "about a boy who went walking in the mountains with his dog. They found one of the places where the spirits live, and they saw them dancing there. The dog came back, but the boy didn't. The dog found the boy's family, and he led them back into the mountains. They found the dancers again, only this time there was one more dancer than before. The dog went up to the new dancer, and the dancer scratched him on the head, as if he knew the dog—which he did. He was the same boy, transformed into a spirit by staying too long with the others." Ricky stared straight at Callie. "The *Gahn* meant well and all, but the two worlds just don't belong together."

Callie remembered how, the morning before,

her hand had passed straight through her face. Was she turning into a ghost, just like the boy in the story? She shivered, pulling her arms tightly around herself.

"Besides," Ricky said, pointing at Star, "that horse doesn't look like any sort of good spirit. She just looks like a regular ghost, a horse who died. Ghosts can't even try to help you. They cause trouble just because of what they are."

Callie grew angry again, and anger dissolved her fear. "Star isn't trouble," she yelled, her cheeks growing hot. "You don't understand. You don't—you don't know her at all!"

"I don't *want* to know her," Ricky yelled back. Callie thought bitterly that he didn't want to know anyone who wasn't already familiar to him, who he didn't think belonged. "If you had any sense," Ricky said, "you'd ignore that horse completely and hope she goes away."

Callie turned furiously away from him, back to Star. Star was breathing hard again, making the same awful wheezing sound she had earlier. Callie felt a sudden burst of fear from the mare. As she watched, Star's legs buckled beneath her, and she collapsed to the ground. This time, she didn't even try to get up again, just stared wearily at Callie.

"Star!" Callie screamed.

The horse shimmered, then all at once disappeared completely. Callie reached for Star's presence—and screamed again. The corner of her mind, the place where Star so often was, felt completely empty.

Callie threw herself at the space where Star had been, expecting to grasp only air. Instead, her arms went firmly around Star's neck. For a moment she saw just the faintest image of the horse—a flash of mane, a swish of tail, a prickling of the ears. Then Star turned solid beneath her. The mare stood once more, and Callie stood beside her. Callie felt Star's happiness, pure joy at the two of them being together. Callie pressed her cheek against Star's silky shoulder. Star was here. Everything was all right.

She had a sudden, lurching feeling, as if she and Star were being pulled through a wall of ice. The gray tendrils at the edges of Callie's vision lunged forward, filling her entire sight. Clammy moisture got down beneath her shirt, spread through her whole body. The ground felt strange beneath her feet, spongy and not quite solid. Callie clutched Star's neck and looked around.

She was surrounded by a swirling gray landscape. Her backyard was completely gone, and there was no sky, only mist. The air was damp and musty, like a room left shut up for too long. Very far away, she thought she heard someone call her name, but she didn't see any-one. After a moment, the voice was gone.

Callie swallowed, fighting panic. The gray had taken her; she'd disappeared for real.

And this time, there was no one to draw her back again.

Chapter Ten

Callie felt chilled, cold and clammy, like she'd never get warm again. She released her hold on Star and rubbed her arms, but the chill wouldn't go away. Voices moaned in the distance, much louder than before, and somehow the sound made Callie even colder. Far away, through the mist, she saw shadowy figures, stretching long, gray arms toward her. She moved closer to Star, suddenly desperate for the horse's warmth.

Star nudged Callie's shoulder. "Do you know where we are?" Callie asked. Star just leaned toward Callie. Callie felt comfort and calm from the mare, as if this were the most normal place in the world to be. Maybe for Star it was. Was this where Star went, when she wasn't with Callie?

Star's calm made Callie calmer, too. She looked into Star's dark eyes. Star looked back; Callie felt her love as strongly as ever.

What she didn't feel from Star was tiredness, or confusion, or loneliness. Callie looked at Star harder. The horse's scratches were gone;

her hair wasn't tangled or matted with dirt. Her breathing was ordinary and quiet. Her nose and eyes weren't even running. She shone, as brightly as she ever had, much more silver than gray.

"You're all right!" Callie said. All traces of Star's illness were gone. Callie felt Star's happiness rise to match her own. The horse's ears twitched cheerfully about. Callie threw her arms around Star and hugged her. She suddenly didn't care that she was in some strange, ghostly place. Star was all right. She really was. Callie wanted to shout, to dance, to run around in circles.

Star nudged Callie's chest. What Star wanted, more than anything, was to ride.

Callie wanted to ride, too. The three days since she'd last ridden seemed ages ago now. She put her foot in Star's stirrup, and she swung onto Star's back, more lightly and gracefully than she ever had before. Star's hair felt cool and silky against her bare legs. She took the reins in her hand.

Gallop, Callie thought.

Star broke into her four-beat run, racing through the damp mist. There was no dirt to kick up beneath Star's feet, no wind to brush Callie's cheek, but still Callie could tell they were running faster than ever before. Her breath caught in her throat. Happiness bubbled up in her.

With nothing but gray all around them, Callie felt more than ever like they were flying instead of running, soaring through the cool mist. Callie never wanted to land, never wanted to touch ground again.

The shadowy figures moved closer. They reached out to Callie, but she was flying too fast; their icy fingers only touched her lightly, and then were left behind. No one could catch her, not now.

She no longer minded the cold, no longer minded the swirling mist all around her. If anything, the mist felt soft, comfortable. Moisture brushed Callie's cheek. She dropped Star's reins; she didn't really need them, anyway. She felt almost sleepy, in spite of how fast Star flew. She'd slept so little the past few days. Her eyes were heavy; she let them shut. Instead of darkness, the gray remained, even behind closed lids.

Was she sliding, losing her hold on Star's back? The dampness cushioned her, and she couldn't tell for sure. She thought she felt herself falling, down through soft, damp mist. She knew she should be scared, but she wasn't. Her thoughts were strange and slow, like her head was filled with cotton.

She couldn't tell when she landed, but after a while she felt Star's nose urgently nudging her chest. She felt the horse's worry. *I'm fine,*

Callie wanted to say, but her tongue was as heavy as her eyelids. Instead, she thought the words. She and Star were together; that was all that really mattered.

Star kept nudging at Callie; Callie wasn't sure why. She tried to stand, but that took far too much effort. She sank back down. Lying there was so much easier than trying to move, so much more comfortable. The moaning voices started up again—had they ever stopped?—and now, Callie could make out the words. *Wait*, they said. *Rest.* Resting sounded like a good idea to Callie.

Star nickered, a sharp, warning sound. That woke Callie up a little. Why was Star worried? She wasn't sure, but maybe she should find out. She forced her eyes open, saw that the shadowy figures had moved close to her again. She started to sit up. Shadow hands shoved against her, trying to keep her down. Star nickered once more, and Callie forced herself to push against those hands and sit upright. It took almost more effort than she could manage. Afterward she just sat there for a while, breathing hard.

The mist had thickened into fog, so dense that Callie barely saw her own hands in front of her. Star's dark eyes glowed through the gray. Around her, Callie saw other eyes glowing, too. Star kept nudging Callie, urging her to

stand. Sitting was hard enough, though. Callie
wanted to lie back down again, to curl up in
the fog for a while.

Stop, the voices around her moaned. *Sleep*.
She couldn't tell whether the voices came from
the shadowy figures or not. She couldn't remember why she'd found them so frightening
before.

Very far away, Callie heard something else.
Star's ears perked forward. Someone was calling Callie's name, in a voice much sharper
than the moaning around her. Callie followed
Star's gaze, squinting out through the gray. At
first she didn't see anything. Then, very faintly,
she made out two figures, somewhere beyond
the fog, figures that were somehow more solid
and less shadowy than those all around her.
Callie didn't know who they were. She didn't
care. They didn't have anything to do with her.
She turned back to Star.

Star snorted and pushed up against Callie's
shoulder. Callie looked out again.

"Callie?" one of the new figures called. Callie knew the voice, but for several moments
couldn't remember the name that went with
it. The figure called again, and Callie realized
it was Amy. She sounded scared. Callie wanted
to tell her that everything was all right, that
there was nothing to be frightened of, but she
still couldn't talk.

"I know she's out there," Amy said. "If I focus right, I can almost see her."

"I told her," someone else, a boy, said. It was Ricky. "I told her that you can't mess with this stuff."

Despite the comfortable fog, despite how sleepy she was, Callie felt herself getting angry. Ever since she'd met Ricky he'd been saying obnoxious things, acting like she didn't know what she was talking about. She was sick of it. Anger made her face hot, pushed the cold and the fog back a little.

"Stupid," Ricky muttered. "Why'd she have to be such an idiot?"

"She's not an idiot," Amy said, sounding defensive.

"Then why's she acting like one?" Ricky demanded. "Why'd she let herself get into this mess? Why'd she ever have to bother with that stupid old horse?"

Callie felt the anger rise more strongly in her; the ghostly figures around her seemed to back away in response. Why couldn't Ricky just leave her alone? "Star's not stupid!" she said. "And neither am I, whatever you think!" Her voice was startlingly loud. It cut through the fog and the cold, and it cut through the cotton, too. All of a sudden, she could think a bit more clearly.

"I heard something." Amy's voice, very low.

"Yeah," Ricky whispered. "Me too." His voice sounded strange, worried. He seemed almost glad to have heard her, which didn't make any sense at all.

Callie grew even angrier, furious. She glared at Ricky through the fog, even though she could still barely see him. She wished he would just go away. She never wanted to hear his voice again.

The heat in her face spread like fire through the rest of her body, making the damp cold back off some more. Callie looked at herself, sitting in the fog, gray tendrils and strange ghostly figures swirling all around her. She started trembling. What was going on? What was she doing here? Everything had seemed all right a moment before.

She found enough energy to reach up and grab one of Star's stirrups. She clutched it tightly, and she pulled herself to her feet. She stood there, holding Star and breathing hard.

Callie remembered how Star had been wheezing, out in the yard, how her breathing had been so strained. She remembered how exhausted Star had felt—as exhausted as Callie felt now. Had fighting that weariness been what had made Star sick? Yet Star hadn't gotten tired as quickly as Callie had; they'd been together for a while before the problems began.

Was the ghost world much more tiring to humans than the human world was to ghosts?

The worlds just don't belong together, Ricky had said. In Callie's world, Star got tired and ill. Now that they were in this ghostly gray place, Star was fine, but Callie was worn out. Already she felt her anger weakening, felt her arms and legs growing heavy. She forced a leg up into the stirrup. Her whole body was like lead, but she gripped Star's mane and saddle and dragged herself up onto the horse's back.

She felt her thoughts slowing down again, watched the fog thickening, saw the ghostly figures growing close enough to touch her once more. Amy and Ricky shimmered and began to fade, disappearing somewhere behind the gray. Callie stared after them, but they didn't come back. She listened for Amy's voice, or even Ricky's, but heard nothing. She tried to call out to them, but her tongue remained heavy and thick.

Now what am I going to do? she wondered. Star snorted, as if picking up on the thought. She turned her head around to look at Callie. Callie felt the horse's love, and beneath it, her concern.

You got me here, Callie thought. *Can you get me home, too?* Star's ears perked up, as if considering that.

Callie pictured her yard, with its trampled

dirt, rusty fences, and dry wash. She pictured her house, Amy and Ricky standing beside it. She pictured the bright blue sky and the sharp, jagged outline of the Catalina Mountains. The images started to fade into gray, but Callie forced them back and clung to them.

For a second Star hesitated. Then she started forward, first at a slow walk, then faster. She broke into a trot, a canter, a gallop, and beyond all those gaits into something that felt faster still, faster than anything Callie could describe. Clammy hands grabbed Callie and were ripped away. The moans rose into wailing, piercing screams.

Callie and Star hit the wall of ice with a shattering crash. Slivers of cold sliced through Callie's skin, cutting her, numbing her. She tried to scream, but her mouth froze. Her whole body turned to ice, and then the world went white.

Chapter Eleven

She was cold, painfully cold. The cold burned, sharp as knives, through her hands and feet. She tried to open her eyes, but the lids wouldn't move. She was still frozen.

"I feel a pulse," someone said. Was it Amy? She sounded sharp and brittle. Maybe that was because of the cold, too. "And she's breathing."

"But her skin's all icy," Ricky said. His voice sounded scared, no hint of laughter in it now.

Someone rubbed Callie's hand, sending daggers through her palm. *Stop it*, she wanted to say, *that hurts*, but her mouth was frozen shut.

"I'm calling 911," Amy said. Callie heard her running away from them.

At least Callie's thoughts were clear, with the same sharp clarity as the cold. She reached out for Star and felt the horse's worried presence reach back. At the touch of Star's thoughts the cold began to melt. Or maybe that was because of whoever was still rubbing her hand.

Warmth spread through her. There was a moment of incredible pain; Callie's lips thawed out, and she screamed. She opened her eyes to bright blue desert sky. The sun burned. Callie shut her eyes again. Around her, hot wind blew.

"She's alive!" Ricky yelled. Callie couldn't believe how relieved he sounded. She heard Amy, who must have still been nearby, turn around and run back toward them.

She was lying on her back, on hard, rocky ground. Callie opened her eyes again, and she saw that she was in her own backyard, not far from the wash. She was still cold, but it was a normal sort of cold, what she'd feel on an autumn day back East. Ricky knelt by her side, rubbing her hand. Callie looked at him and he let go, as if suddenly embarrassed.

Amy ran across the yard and knelt by Callie's other side. "You're back," she said. She repeated the words, as if unable to believe them. "You came back."

Callie looked around for Star, found her standing just a few yards away. She started to sit up, but dizziness washed over her and she had to lie down again.

"Take it slow," Amy said.

Callie nodded. She lay still for a few seconds. Someone had draped a jacket—Ricky's denim jacket—over her. She took it off, sat up more slowly, and breathed deeply. Dry desert air moved easily in and out of her lungs. Nothing had ever felt so wonderful. The awful tiredness was gone, too, and she could think clearly. She looked straight at Star. *You brought me home,* Callie thought. Star looked back, through worried eyes. *I'm all right,* Callie told her.

"We didn't think we were ever going to see you again," Amy said. Ricky nodded. Wind blew his long hair into his face. Callie was still kind of surprised that he cared one way or the other.

"You barely made it back," Amy said. "I don't know how you did. I mean, we saw you and Star standing there, but you were so faint, so far away from us. Then there was this weird gray wall, and you and Star ran through it, and you fell from her saddle . . ." Amy gripped Callie's hand tightly.

"You got lucky," Ricky said, but his voice was less sharp than usual.

"If it were me," Amy said softly, "I'm not sure I could have come back." Callie looked at her, not sure what she was talking about.

"I mean," Amy said, "if I'd been able to ride Star through that wall, to my parents somehow, I'm not sure I could have left them again. I only wanted to see them for a few minutes, to talk to them . . ." Her voice trailed off, and she took a deep breath. "But you had so much trouble getting back that I'm not sure I would have made it at all.

"I think," Amy said slowly, "that even if Mom and Dad can see me and hear me and all the rest, they must know how hard it is for people to go back and forth. Even if they could come here to see me, the way Star keeps coming to see you, I don't think they would. They'd want to protect me, you know? To keep me from getting trapped, like you almost did." Amy's expression turned determined. "I have no way of knowing for sure whether that's true. But I'm going to believe it, anyway."

"Your parents always were pretty sensible," Ricky said, and Callie remembered that he'd known them. For just a moment, his face went dark. Then he smiled, a bit sadly, at Amy. "It's the sort of thing they would do, I think."

Callie looked at Amy and Ricky. They'd helped bring her home, too, as much as Star had. If she hadn't heard their voices, she never would have made it back. If she hadn't gotten angry at Ricky—Callie started to laugh. Who would have thought she'd ever be grateful for that? Laughing dissolved the last of the cold, leaving her with only the normal heat of Tucson in August. Amy and Ricky looked at her as though she were crazy. But Star snorted, and Callie knew she was laughing, too.

"Are you okay?" Amy asked.

Still laughing, Callie nodded. "The only way to cope with something serious is to laugh a little, you know? Besides," she said, looking straight at Ricky, "if you can't take a joke . . ."

Amy giggled. And to Callie's surprise, Ricky grinned, then burst into laughter himself. "Not bad, Callie from New York," he said, and laughed harder.

"Callie from Tucson," she said, correcting him. Even if she had just moved here, this was still her home. She belonged here, every bit as much as Star belonged in the ghostly gray place she'd just escaped. In a way she'd known that for a while now, but waking up to that bright blue sky, to the familiar sun on her arms, had reminded her. She wasn't an outsider, whatever anyone said. And she loved the desert, with all its heat and dust. She didn't want to change it any more than she had to. That counted for something, didn't it?

Star walked up to join them, nudging Callie with her wet nose. Callie looked at her. Already the horse's nose and eyes were running. Callie felt Star's tiredness, and it reminded her of what she'd felt in Star's ghostly world. She bit her lip, cutting the laughter short. Callie wanted Star to stay with her, but Star couldn't, any more than Callie could have stayed in Star's world. Maybe it was the conflict between those things—wanting to stay but needing to go—that had made Star sick in the first place.

Callie took hold of Amy's shoulder and, leaning heavily on her friend, pulled herself to her feet. She felt another wave of dizziness and waited for it to subside. Then she walked over to Star and leaned on her. Ricky winced.

"Don't worry," Callie said. "I'm not planning on leaving with her again."

"You didn't plan to leave the first time." Ricky's voice was harsh—or maybe just worried; Callie couldn't quite tell. "Don't you get it yet? Ghosts are dangerous. We shouldn't have anything to do with them."

Callie still couldn't accept that, even though she knew how dangerous Star's world was and didn't want to go back there, not ever. She wondered who all the ghostly figures she'd seen were, why they'd been trying to make her stay. Did they even know how dangerous her staying would have been? She wondered whether Michael, Star's original owner, was somewhere among them. She wondered whether Amy's parents were there, too. Callie shuddered, not sure she wanted to know. It'd been hard enough to pull away without knowing who any of the figures were.

But for all that, she still didn't believe that she and Star shouldn't have anything to do with each other, that they never should have met.

She thought about the mountain spirits, about how they'd gotten tired of living with people and had decided to leave. The story didn't say that they shouldn't have come, only that they couldn't stay.

Star wasn't a mountain spirit, but the ghost of a horse that had been alive once. Still, nothing changed the fact that Star had helped Callie in so many ways, and that Callie had helped her.

Callie thought about the boy who'd gone into the mountains and never come back. Maybe his mistake hadn't been finding the spirits, but staying with them too long. Callie wasn't sure Ricky would agree, and she wasn't sure the story was meant to say anything like that at all. But she couldn't help wondering what would have happened if the boy had left with the dog, instead of lingering behind. Amy had seen her parents briefly, too, just after they'd died, and that had been all right, even though she couldn't see them again.

"I think," Callie said slowly, "that it's fine for ghosts and people to be together sometimes, if they're careful and don't stay too long." Ricky opened his mouth to protest, but before he could say anything, Callie added, "And right now, I also think it's time—past time—for Star to leave." She swallowed hard, hating the words yet knowing they were true. Already Star's breathing was heavier than before. Callie suspected Star would stay if she asked her to, but she couldn't. She couldn't let Star get sick all over again.

Callie hugged Star tightly. She ran her hands along Star's muscled shoulders, through her mane, over her soft hair, up between her ears. She tried to memorize her silky feel, her sweet cut-grass smell, the bottomless depths of her eyes. She focused on the feel of Star's mind in her own. *I love you*, Callie thought. She felt Star's love in return, solid and strong.

Amy walked up and patted Star on the shoulder, silently saying good-bye herself. Then, without a word, she stepped back again, leaving Callie and Star alone.

Callie took a deep breath. Then she pushed Star gently away.

At first Star wouldn't leave. Callie felt a pang of loneliness from the horse, felt the same unbearable loneliness in herself. It took all the strength Callie had, even more strength than she'd needed to climb onto Star's back in the gray landscape, to whisper, "Go. You can't stay here."

Star turned and took one tentative step, then another, away from Callie and the wash, toward her corral. Only it wasn't her corral anymore. Soon, people would come to start digging the pool for real, whether Callie wanted them to or not.

Callie stepped after Star. She only wanted to see where Star was going, to maybe say good-bye one more time.

Ricky reached out and grasped her hand, pulling her back. Callie let him. She told herself she wouldn't have followed Star any farther, but she wasn't sure.

Star burst into a gallop, full of fiery grace. She looked healthy again, her coat glistening bright silver against the stark desert sky. By the time Star reached what used to be her corral, Callie could see right through her. A moment later she was gone, leaving Callie behind, without even hoofprints to show where she'd been.

The bond between Callie and Star snapped, like a rope frayed through, and was gone. Callie's mind held nothing but her own thoughts.

"Good-bye," Callie whispered. She took a deep breath, fighting not to cry.

As she did, she felt something—a tingling down her spine, and love so solid she could almost touch it. After a moment the feeling faded, but didn't quite go away. Star wasn't completely gone after all. Joy bubbled up within Callie. She started laughing again. Did she feel Star's presence laughing back? She didn't know, but she thought so. Feeling Star there made her suddenly hopeful, made her wonder whether there'd be other times and places where they could visit each other, if only for a short while.

"She's an incredible horse," Amy said, a wistful edge to her voice.

Ricky didn't say anything at all. Instead, he tugged on Callie's hand again; he hadn't let go of it. Was he still worried that Callie would try to leave somehow?

Farther away, in front of the house, Callie heard a car pull into the driveway. Was Mom or Dad already home, or was that just Melissa? How long had Callie been gone?

She realized that sooner or later she'd have to tell her parents she'd left school. Her stomach tightened into a guilty knot. She'd have to think up one more excuse—for better or worse, probably her last excuse—to keep people from finding out about Star. She wasn't sure what she'd say, but somehow, she'd explain what she'd done and deal with it. Maybe Amy and Ricky could help her.

Callie stared at the spot where Star had been a moment more. Then, still feeling Star's love, she turned back to her friends—and to her own desert world.

About the Author

JANNI LEE SIMNER grew up on Long Island and has been working her way west ever since. Unlike Callie Fern, she took nearly a decade crossing the Midwest, spending much of it in St. Louis. She currently lives in Tucson, where she enjoys horseback riding and hiking in the mountains that surround the city. She has published short stories in nearly two dozen magazines and anthologies, including *Starfarer's Dozen* and *Bruce Coville's Book of Nightmares*, *Book of Magic*, and *Book of Aliens II*. The *Phantom Rider* books are her first novels.